THAT BLACK DAY

First published in 2000
by Mercier Press
5 French Church St Cork
E.mail: books@mercier.ie

16 Hume Street Dublin 2
Tel: (01) 661 5299; Fax: (01) 661 8583
E.mail: books@marino.ie

Trade enquiries to CMD Distribution
55A Spruce Avenue
Stillorgan Industrial Park
Blackrock County Dublin
Tel: (01) 294 2556; Fax: (01) 294 2564
E.mail: cmd@columba.ie

© Bill Wall 2000

ISBN 1 85635 325 7

10 9 8 7 6 5 4 3 2 1

A CIP record for this title is available
from the British Library

Cover design by Penhouse Design
Printed in Ireland by ColourBooks,
Baldoyle Industrial Estate, Dublin 13

THAT BLACK DAY

A LUSITANIA STORY

BILL WALL

MERCIER PRESS

A foaming tide
Whitened afar with surge, fan-formed and wide,
Burst from a great door marred by many a blow
From mace and sword and pole-axe, long ago
When gods and giants warred.

'The Wanderings of Oisin'
W. B. Yeats (1889)

CONTENTS

LUSITANIA

The Cunard liner Lusitania *left New York on 1 May 1915. Just after lunch on Sunday 7 May 1915, near the Old Head of Kinsale, a torpedo from a German U-boat struck her. The ship foundered in less than twenty minutes. One thousand, one hundred and ninety-five men, women and children died . . .*

Monday 1 May 1915

Connie

Sarah Moore stood head and shoulders above the crowd, but still she could not see her way to the gangway. She was a magnificent woman, proud and strong, with a mane of red hair that told of her Irish ancestry, but with the frank, determined eyes of one born in America. Holding tightly to her right hand, little Oisín kept his inherited red head down, watching the big boots that swirled on either side of him. One of those could make a pretty bruise on his foot if he let himself get in their way. On the other side young Connie, dark-eyed and intense, was more concerned about the box she was carrying. It contained a new hat, given to her in Boston by her great-aunt Elizabeth, a tremendous old lady who smoked cigars and wrote detective stories in news-papers. 'That hat,' Great-Aunt Elizabeth told her, 'is a first-class original wild-west hat. I am told it was worn by Billy the Kid himself. Before he was shot, of course.' It came in a fine hard box, she said, and would easily last the journey to Ireland. 'Though heaven knows, once you get back to the old country you will find that the rain and the damp will ruin it unless you keep it in a warm room.' Connie promised that she would take care of it and her great-aunt Elizabeth laughed aloud, saying, 'Lord's sake, child, it's for wearing! It's not a family treasure!' But for Connie, it was indeed a treasure, a memento of her mother's family, all the people she had met in Boston and Newport and the other places she had visited, people she might not meet again for many years. It had been a wonderful and exciting trip. The vastness of America had overwhelmed her: the distances, the size of everything. And the welcome they had received was just as big. Everywhere they went there were parties, boating trips, picnics, excursions to this or that place of interest for the visitors from Ireland. Connie thought that the hearts of her American cousins were as big as the continent itself.

But now it was time to go home, and Connie was drowning in the noise and crush of the waterfront. Thousands of people were talking at once. There was weeping and cheering, and then a long blast on the ship's sirens, deafening almost, like a train blowing its whistle right in her ear. Then the crowd thinned out and Connie's box was no longer in danger and Oisín had let his mother's hand go and was running forward, and there was the gangway and an officer in a smart uniform checking their boarding passes. After nine weeks in America, Connie was delighted to hear the soft Irish accent of the officer directing them to their cabin.

'My goodness,' Sarah said to him, 'what a crowd! How do you manage at all?'

The officer shook his head. 'Not so many this time, madam. Not so many people travelling to Europe with the war on.'

'Did you see the notice in the newspaper?' Oisín said, his eyes shining with excitement. 'The Germans put a notice in the newspaper, saying they would sink the *Lusitania* with torpedoes. My sister Connie read it to me. I'm not in reading class yet, you know. Did you see that notice?'

The officer squatted down so that his face was looking straight into Oisín's. 'Don't you worry about that, young chap,' he said. 'This liner's too fast for the Germans. The submarine hasn't been built yet that could catch us in a chase. And if any submarine did come near, they'd have this to answer to.' He made a big fist and held it up to Oisín's gaze. 'I've rapped many a German on the nose with this one!'

They all laughed. Suddenly the anxiety of the last few days – the hurry to pack, the worry about reaching New York in time for the sailing, the crowd and the noise – just faded away, and it was a holiday again. The other passengers in the ship were happy and excited. The crowds were waving. The whole length of Fourteenth Street was packed with carriages and hackneys, motor cars and coaches, and everywhere the milling, cheering, waving, weeping crowds.

Sarah Moore fussed over her ticket and eventually found someone who could direct them to their cabins. Oisín seemed somewhat cowed by the whole affair now, the bustle and rush of everything. He stood to one side while the sailor gave directions to his mother, and made faces at Connie, but they were only half-hearted faces. There was no real insult in them.

'I'd like to stay on deck. May I?' Connie asked.

Her mother nodded her head distractedly. 'Don't stray, dear. Stay up here. We'll come back when we've settled our baggage in. You be careful now.'

On the far side of the ship there was peace and quiet. The tugs had their hawsers made fast and were ready at a moment's notice to pull the great liner off the pier. Their engines puffed little jets of steam into the warm May air. Their captains stood on their tiny bridges, each smoking a pipe contentedly and waiting for the signal from the liner. This was the side that Connie preferred. She let her mother and Oisín go below to find their cabin and explore the ship. Oisín would want to see everything. He would eventually escape from his mother, as he always did, and rush up and down the passageways, bumping into passengers and annoying the crew. Connie knew that such behaviour was only to be expected from a nine-year-old boy. By staying on deck away from it all she hoped to show that she was *not* nine years of age, and definitely not a boy! She was a very serious thirteen, and believed that she had an understanding of the world that was as good as (or better than) her mother's. And one thing she knew for certain was that nine-year-old boys were trouble!

'Hello, young lady, why aren't you watching the excitement?' It was the young Irish officer who had checked her ticket. He had come up to the rail she was leaning against, his peaked cap pulled low over his eyes to keep the sun out.

'I prefer a little peace and quiet,' Connie said grandly, and immediately felt proud, and very grown up. Yes, she did prefer a little peace and quiet. It was like something her mother would say.

'I'm of your mind entirely,' the officer said. 'All that noise!'

Connie looked closely at the officer's face to see if he was joking. Adults had an annoying habit of treating everything she said as hilariously funny. They had a way of raising their eyebrows and putting their hands to their faces to cover their smiles. But the officer was quite serious.

'Is that why you've come to this side?' she asked.

'No, miss. I'm afraid I'm on official business. It's my job to keep an eye on those blasted tugboats out there, to make sure that they don't do anything wrong. A ship this big can do an awful lot of damage if she doesn't do exactly what we want her to do.'

Connie was interested. It suddenly occurred to her that perhaps she could become a ship's officer when she grew up. She would get to wear that splendid uniform – but how could she! She could never wear trousers, and she had never seen an officer in a skirt. She almost laughed at the thought, but restrained herself.

'Is it a lot of trouble to get the ship ready?'

The officer smiled. 'Indeed it is. What would you say if I told you that we have taken aboard – this very morning, mind – two hundred barrels of oysters fresh from Connecticut, brought up by the night train? Or what about nearly half a million pounds of beef and bacon? Every bit of that has to be stowed away. And mark my words, there won't be a bite of it left at the end of the voyage and we'll have to start all over again. And it's all very well here in New York. You can get the best of everything, and all very reasonable. But fancy what it'll be like at home? Everything is short. No sugar, no tea, all the beef and bacon gone to the army or the navy. No it's not an easy thing to get a ship like this ready for sea.'

'And it's not so easy to get oysters in England, with the war and everything.'

He smiled. 'Oh yes. There won't be any more oysters until the war ends, whenever that may be. The quality will have to make do with periwinkles on the way back!' He laughed loudly at his own joke. But Connie put on her tragic face and gazed out at the sparkling water. 'Father is at the war,' she said. 'He was a volunteer. One of Mr Redmond's volunteers.'

'I see,' the officer said. Suddenly he turned to Connie and stretched out a hand. 'Regan is my name,' he said. 'Patrick Regan. And who might you be yourself?'

'Connie . . . Constance Moore,' she said.

'I'm delighted to meet you, Miss Moore.' They smiled at each other.

'Are you a captain?' Connie asked.

'Indeed I'm not. I'm a humble third officer. What they used to call a third mate once. But on the Cunard Line we don't call them mates at all. Not grand enough.'

'Father is a captain.'

'Is he now? Is it a soldier he is?'

'Yes. Well, he started as a soldier. Then they asked if he could ride a horse and of course he could because he had lots of horses before the war. So they put him in the Flying Corps, and now he's a flier.' Flying was such a dashing way to fight a war, Connie thought, high up above the trenches where the air was clean and fresh. Her father told her that, in fact, he did very little fighting, that most of his time was taken up flying observers over enemy lines so that they could report on troop movements. Once or twice he had been shot at but he had never needed to fire back. So he *told* her, but she guessed that it was a lot more dangerous than that. Her father would try to reassure her, make her think that everything was easy, that there was no danger.

'In an aeroplane?'

'Yes. He's pretty good at it too, I can tell you. He showed me how it's done once, when he was home on leave. I think I might be a flier when I grow up.' If I don't become a ship's officer, Connie thought.

Now the young man did smile. 'I'd say a pretty girl such as you will find a handsome man to marry, and then you won't have to be anything at all. Don't bother your head with things like that.'

'Mother says that girls may be anything they like in the modern age. She's a suffragette.' Connie was angry at his suggestion. Two pink spots about the size of pennies had appeared on her cheeks and her hands were clenched tightly on the ship's rail. Patrick Regan noticed none of that.

'What's a suffragette? Hey! Watch that hawser!' Patrick Regan suddenly sprang to the ladder that led up to the boat-deck and was gone before Connie could explain what the word meant. She heard him shouting orders to the tugboats from up there and she was sure that he was using a loudspeaker, his voice was so loud. She was also sure that even if she had been able to find the right words, Patrick Regan would not have understood, because he was a man, and most men did not believe that women could be their equals at anything but cooking and sewing. Her father was different. He believed that women should have the vote and have the right to work at any job they wanted. One day it will happen, he was always saying. Connie believed him. She was preparing her mind for that day. She had no intention of being something ordinary.

When Connie thought of her father she always pictured him sitting in his aeroplane high up above the clouds where he said everything was bright and sunny. She imagined the breeze in his face, and the sun gleaming on the wings of his aeroplane. Sometimes he sang to himself when he was up there. He had said so. She liked to think of him like that because it kept the nightmares out of her thoughts. She had terrible nightmares. She saw his aeroplane falling out of the sky, wrapped in a ball of fire. Or he was jumping out, a mile above the ground, and falling, falling, until he was shattered into a thousand pieces. Or sometimes she dreamed that a German bullet went straight through the thin cloth that covered the aeroplane and straight through her father's heart. That was a terrible dream because she saw him dying there in his lonely place far above the green fields and quiet villages of France, far from his home and his family and the land that he loved.

Connie had come to believe that the newspapers in America were only able to find out-of-date news. It stood to reason. If something happened in Flanders or Picardy where the war was, or further away on the Eastern Front where Germany was fighting Russia, the news had to come to England first. Then it had to be sent to America, all the way across the Atlantic. The Atlantic was such a vast ocean. So it had come into her head that, when they returned to Ireland, she would hear that the war had been over for weeks, unknown to the American newspapers, that her father and all his comrades would have returned from the Western Front, all hale and hearty, and that her father would be waiting at the door of Ballyshane House. Sometimes the picture was so real that she could see the brown boots he wore when he went riding, and the tweed jacket that he loved. She could smell the pipesmoke-smell that was always around him. She could hear his voice. 'Welcome home, sweethearts,' he would say and hug them all one by one, and then they would go in, and send news to May in the kitchen that she should make tea and send up some of her soda bread with a large plate of butter. At first that thought had made her happy, but now as the time drew nearer and she knew that in a few days she would be standing at that very door herself, she thought of it in fear. What if the war weren't over after all? Or worse, what if there was a telegram from the King to say that Father had been wounded? She could not think beyond that because if she did it would lead her backwards into the world of her worst nightmares.

Now the boat was pulling slowly away from the Fourteenth Street pier. She was like a huge whale rippling sideways and backwards, and Connie could feel the whale's heart-throb through the planks of the deck, the great engines that drove her thousands of miles at such wonderful speed. Behind her, the *Lusitania's* four enormous funnels, each as tall as a church spire, were belching smoke and small sparks. Out in the Hudson River, a little tugboat was puffing a cloud of steam as it towed a barge loaded with barrels. It reminded Connie of the Guinness barges she had seen once on the Royal Canal, near Dublin. But the name on the stern said 'Heywood – New York'. She waved, and a sailor who had been watching the ship waved back, lifting his cap off his head and twirling it high in the air. He seemed to be in a joyous mood and he had good reason to be on this fine May day, guiding his boat in the warm sunshine.

Connie watched the pushing and pulling of the tugs that looked as tiny as drifting matchsticks on the sea below. She wondered if the Germans really meant to torpedo the *Lusitania*. She had seen the notice herself. 'Travellers intending to embark on the Atlantic voyage,' it said, 'are reminded that a state of war exists between Germany and her allies and Great Britain and her allies: that the zone of war includes the waters adjacent to the British Isles: that, in accordance with formal notice given by the Imperial German Government, vessels flying the flag of Great Britain or any of her allies are liable to destruction in those waters and that travellers sailing in the war zone on ships of Great Britain or her allies do so at their own risk.'

The notice was from the Imperial German Embassy in Washington. On the train up from Boston everyone had been talking about it. One lady said that no one would sink a shipful of passengers. It simply wasn't done. A clergyman, who spent most of the journey deep in an old black-covered copy of the Bible, gave it as his opinion that the end of the world was near when such things were happening. A man in a white suit who said he was from Alabama told them that you couldn't trust foreigners.

But Connie remembered her father's words to her before he went off to the war. 'The Germans are just like ourselves,' he had said. 'There's good and bad in everyone.'

Now Connie was hoping that it was the good Germans who were out there in the Atlantic, the ones who would never torpedo a passenger ship and kill thousands of people, and that the bad ones had gone off duty and were safely at home in their beds in Germany.

Tuesday 2 May 1915

U-20

'Alarm! Alarm!' The shout echoed through the hull. There were running footsteps everywhere, the sound of hatches slamming, orders from the control room being repeated among the crew. Oberleutnant Walter Schwieger was out of his bunk almost before the second shout reached his tiny cabin. He always slept fully dressed except for his tunic, cap and boots. It was the work of a moment to pull these on.

Now the pilot, Otto Lanz, was reporting, standing to attention as rigidly as was possible in the bucking, twisting, low-ceilinged U-boat, his neck bent like a listening robin's.

'Ship, *Herr Oberleutnant*. Hull down almost over the horizon. Moving slowly towards us. I have taken the precaution of readying the boat for diving, *Herr Oberleutnant*.'

'Flag?'

'Stars and stripes, *Herr Oberleutnant*! So we think.'

Walter Schwieger cursed under his breath.

'What do you think?'

'False colours, *Herr Oberleutnant.* There are very few American ships here. Besides, I have a feeling . . . '

Walter Schwieger knew his pilot's 'feelings' well. Lanz was an excellent pilot with an uncanny skill in identification, and identification was the most important part of the U-boat war. The oceans were full of ships of different nationalities. Some were allies of Great Britain and therefore Walter Schwieger's enemies. Some were ships of neutral nations who so far had not taken either side, countries like Norway or Denmark or, most importantly, the United States of America. Orders from headquarters always emphasised how important it was not to attack a neutral, and Walter Schwieger knew that if he sank a neutral ship he might be responsible for bringing another nation into the war against his homeland. This ship flying the Stars and Stripes – she could be one of two things. She could be a British ship flying false colours to fool him. If that was what she was, he, Walter Schwieger, had a duty to put a torpedo in her without delay. On the other hand, she might actually be an American, and if he sank her, the United States might enter the war on the British side, and that would be a disaster indeed. Walter Schwieger doubted if his country, after a long year of war, could withstand the arrival of hundreds of thousands of fresh soldiers from America. If that was the result of his torpedo, he would be responsible for the ruin of his beloved homeland.

The responsibility was terrible, but a decision had to be made. During previous voyages he had come to trust in the quiet intelligence of his pilot. They got on well together, the young, intelligent, scholarly pilot and the tough, experienced old sailor. They made a good team, he and Otto Lanz. Now he made an instant decision to trust him again.

'False colours, you think, Lanz? Very good. We will dive.'

Now began the complicated procedure of filling the ship's ballast tanks and submerging. More watertight hatches slammed. Valves were turned. Voices spoke and answered each other. Orders were issued and repeated. There was the hiss of compressed air.

'Both surface engines shut down.'

'Both electric motors ready.'

'Battery state eighty-seven per cent charged; electrolyte level normal in all cells.'

'All compressed air tanks full.'

'Diving tanks clear.'

'Diving rudder clear.'

'Clear to dive, *Herr Oberleutnant*.'

The big diesels went silent and their racket was replaced by the quieter whirring of the electric engines they used when below the surface. Walter Schwieger stood at his post in the control room, listening to the crew he had trained so well go through their appointed tasks. Yes, he thought, I would trust any one of them with my life. Then the thought occurred to him, not for the first time, that this was exactly what he did every time he set out on a patrol, because the survival of a U-boat depended on every single member of the crew. If one man failed to do his duty at a critical time, they would all finish up in a very expensive can of fish food at the bottom of the ocean.

Now the stations were reporting that all was well. Lanz was giving the course they were to steer to the helm. An air of quiet anticipation had settled on the crew, each at his post in their separate rooms, the control room, the engineers, the torpedo room. Thirty men all locked up in a steel barrel. 'We have reached periscope depth, *Herr Oberleutnant*,' Schwieger was told by the man who stood by the depth meter.

Through the periscope Walter Schwieger picked out the distant shape of the ship. It was difficult to get a clear look at it because the sea was quite rough, with a heavy swell running down from the northwest. When running on the surface earlier, the submarine had plunged and reared like a wild horse. Several of the men had been sick, and now the air inside the hull had a faint suggestion of vomit. Besides the rough sea, it was barely daylight, and there were fogbanks about. Only two hours before, steaming in darkness, they had had a bad fright when a destroyer came straight at them, less than three hundred metres away in the fog. There was no time to dive and Walter Schwieger was about to order his crew to prepare to abandon ship when the destroyer turned out to be nothing more than a particularly thick piece of mist.

'What do you think, Otto?'

Walter Schwieger stepped aside to allow Lanz to look.

'Big ship,' Lanz said. 'I will consult my book.'

Walter Schwieger never knew what Lanz meant when he said he would 'consult his book'. It could be the huge Navy identification book that gave pictures, silhouettes and details of every known ship or type of ship in the world. Or it could just as easily be the battered copy of

Homer's *Iliad* which Lanz was translating from Greek into German, because Herr Doktor Otto Lanz had been a scholar of Greek before the war, a graduate of Heidelberg University, a young man marked down for greatness. Walter Schwieger had never lost his admiration for books and people who understood them. A professional naval officer himself, he rarely read anything that wasn't directly related to his job.

Lanz was back at the periscope now, silently mouthing swear words. 'There is fog,' he said. 'She has vanished.'

Walter Schwieger pushed the pilot out of the way and stared into the 'scope. Lanz was right. The ship was gone. A minute ago she was there, steaming towards them, several miles off. The lookout had seen her outlined by the faint light of dawn. Now there was only a grey wall.

'All right,' Walter Schwieger said quietly. 'We will be ready anyway. When we last saw her she was steaming towards us. We will be ready. Perhaps we will get a lucky shot.'

All the way up the North Sea they had played cat and mouse with the Royal Navy. They had encountered several merchant ships, but by bad luck they had been unable to get a shot at anything. Now Walter Schwieger was conscious that his crew needed action. He could sense it in them. He looked around at the ugly steel can that was to be his home for several thousand miles, the walls weeping with condensation already, the smell of bilge water, diesel, vomit and sweat in the air, the pale faces of the men. Yes, they must attack. Success would make the crew a better fighting unit. It would be good for morale.

Every sailor on a U-boat remembered the extraordinary story of Otto Weddigen, commander of *U-9*, who got lost off the coast of Belgium due to a compass failure, and surfaced almost within a stone's throw of three British cruisers, *Aboukir*, *Cressy* and *Hogue*. It was an extraordinary piece of luck, and at that stage of the war, surface ships scarcely believed in U-boats at all. When Weddigen's first torpedo smashed into *Aboukir*, her captain believed she had struck a mine. The other two cruisers immediately stopped to pick up survivors as the *Aboukir* began to sink. Half an hour later, *U-9* was so close to the *Hogue* that they could have thrown the torpedoes at her. Two fish hit her at point-blank range and she began to sink immediately. Not long afterwards *U-9* hit the *Cressy*. She sank in a matter of minutes. Otto Weddigen won the Iron Cross First Class for the action, and the entire crew got the Iron Cross Second Class. They had killed almost 1,400 men and sunk 36,000 tons of shipping. It was every U-boat crew's dream.

Now began the long waiting period when nerves were strung up tight and people's tempers became frayed. On the surface, the diesel engines kept *U-20* moving at a respectable pace, but down here, running on electric engines powered by enormous banks of wet-cell batteries that had to be recharged every few hours, the boat's speed fell away to a mere nine knots. Nine knots! A fast-sailing pleasure yacht could outrun her! Were it not for the fact that they approached their targets unseen, they would never get within range of anything. The slowness of the attack was frustrating at first, but a submarine crew learned to live with it. Patience was the greatest virtue among submariners, greater even than courage. And it was important to keep calm, to listen to the sounds of the ocean, to be quiet.

The ocean is like the strings of a violin and the submarine is the sounding board. Every noise is made louder by the hull. Walter Schwieger had heard whales singing to each other in the high latitudes of the North Atlantic. He had heard dolphins clicking and chattering. He had also heard the whirr of a ship's propellers and the boom-boom-boom of her engines.

He heard them now and immediately he heard the hiss of breath, all along the ship. The crew had stopped breathing for a moment, listening, expecting the target. Now they relaxed a little. They would get their chance.

'Up periscope.'

The fog was lighter again, wispy. It was just possible that they would get a clear shot. He made a guess at where the ship would be when it emerged from the fog and ordered a firing solution to be prepared. Just to be ready. Just in case. Then he ordered torpedoes to be made ready, the torpedo-room crew to be ready to fire. Then he too began to hold his breath.

The faint engine noise grew louder. Big engines. A big ship.

Suddenly she was there, caught in the crosshairs of the periscope. He ordered a new solution. Called for 'Stand by'. The solution came back.

'Los!' he shouted. The order was repeated along the hull. He heard the hiss of compressed air as the torpedo launched. Immediately he heard the torpedo-room officer report one fish gone. Eyes fixed to the periscope, Walter Schwieger called out the details to Otto Lanz. 'About three thousand tons! Merchantman. Two funnels. Flying the Stars and Stripes. Name obscured.'

At the same time he was watching the bubble-track of the torpedo through the water, a white line. It always reminded him of the chalk lines that his teachers had drawn on the blackboard, connecting two points to prove some mathematical theorem. Only now, the theorem was death. If that white line connected with the ship, and if the torpedo had correctly armed itself after launching, dozens of men would die, thousands of tons of supplies for the enemy would sink to the bottom. If the supplies did not reach England, Germany would be stronger and the German army would be able to kill more Britishers. That was the theorem. It made Walter Schwieger tremble, the enormity of that little white chalkline.

'Down 'scope.' He would wait in silence. He would not see that death.

Walter Schwieger was a professional seaman. He took no pleasure in the death of his fellow mariners. If his torpedo struck home he would have done his duty, no more. He would take pride in his skill. But he would also regret the loss of life.

Now the crew were counting. They all knew how long the torpedo should take to strike. Strangely, everyone looked at the roof of the submarine, as if their eyes might penetrate the centimetres of thick steel and thirty feet of ocean, to allow them to see the effect of their work.

'Three, two, one.'

Silence, except for the engine noise. No explosion.

'Up 'scope!'

There she was, now steaming away from them. The torpedo had not hit, or else it had not armed itself. Judging by the ship's behaviour no one aboard her had even seen it.

'Damn!'

He became aware of muttering among the crew. He heard the helmsman say, 'So much for German industry.'

'Silence fore and aft!' Walter Schwieger hissed. 'Rueff, you will not speak of the Fatherland in such a way. Your remark will be noted in the log!'

'I am sorry, *Herr Oberleutnant*,' Gunther Rueff said. 'But we are all so disappointed.'

'Silence!'

And silence did descend on the *U-20*. But it was the silence of depression. Walter Schwieger heard it and knew what it meant. He had heard of U-boats that had cruised three or four thousand miles without a single success. The danger was that they would become desperate. As the time ran out, they would all want to take more risks. In the end, if a U-boat commander lost his caution, he would also lose his boat. Walter Schwieger had lost many friends that way. Even in one year of war the British had destroyed too many submarines.

'Blow the tanks. We will steam on the surface again.'

At least if they were up there on top, it would blow some of this stink out of the hull. It was a nice bright day up there now. The fog was gone. Soon they would be off the coast of Ireland. There would be other ships.

WEDNESDAY 3 MAY 1915

THE GREAT MAN HIMSELF

Connie threw the door of their cabin open and rushed in, all out of breath, her cheeks glowing. 'Mother! Guess who I've seen promenading on the boat-deck!' But her mother was not there. Instead, she stared into the genial, broad face of the steward. He had a bundle of towels over his arm, and she could see that he had just finished tidying the room.

'Who might that be, miss?'

'I was looking for my mother. Have you seen her?'

The steward shook his head. 'I was just tidying things a bit,' he said, as if this explained why he hadn't seen her mother.

'If you see her, will you tell her I have some tremendous news? I'll be on the boat-deck.'

'I certainly will, Miss.'

Again Connie was taken by the uneasy feeling that this adult was not quite taking her seriously. He had an open, pleasant face, but she was quite sure she had seen a smirk on it a moment ago.

'I'm going to tell her that I have seen Sir Hugh Lane,' she said.

'Is that a fact?' the steward said. 'The picture-man, no less.'

Connie was taken aback. She had mentioned the name in the hope of impressing the steward with her superior knowledge.

'Have you heard of him?'

'Sure, the whole country has heard about him,' the steward said. 'Him and the pictures and stuff.'

In the last few moments, Connie had become aware that the steward's accent was Irish. She wondered that out of all the hundreds of people who worked on the *Lusitania*, she had so far only met two Irishmen.

'Where do you come from?'

'Dublin, miss.' The steward began to fold the towels one by one and lay them out on the bed. 'Fresh towels,' he said.

'Did you ever see Mr Yeats?'

The steward shook his head. 'He's not on this deck, miss, I can tell you that. Could be second-class.'

Connie almost laughed. 'Mr Yeats the poet,' she said. 'In Dublin. Mr William Butler Yeats?' The steward shook his head. 'It's many a year now since I was in Dublin. I've been a sailor for the best part of thirty. Anyway, not much to go back for. Not the part where I was born.'

'Mr Yeats,' Connie said, glad at last to have found something that might impress the man, 'is the greatest poet in the world. My mother and father know him. They are always reading his books. My brother is named for one of his poems. 'The Wanderings of Oisín', it is called.'

'Begod, Miss, that same lad is well used to wandering,' the steward said bitterly. 'Do you see this?' He reached into a laundry bag and pulled out one of Oisín's socks. He pointed at a green-black smudge. 'Will you look at that? That's grease! Do you know where that came from? That brother of yours was brought up from the engine room by Leading Stoker Simpson not one hour ago. What was he doing in the engine room, I ask you? That's out of bounds to passengers.'

'He does like to explore,' Connie said lamely, conscious that she had lost the advantage again. 'Mother tells him off, but it doesn't stop him at all.'

'Simpson was in a right stink about it too. About having to come all the way up.'

'I'm sure he didn't mean to break the rules.'

'"Can you get that oil off, Sam?" your mother says to me. But it's not oil at all at all. It's grease.'

'I'd better go back to the boat-deck,' Connie said. 'I've arranged to meet someone.'

The steward seemed to relent. 'Sir Hugh has pictures on board. Did you know? Down in the storage hold. In a box made of lead.'

'Really?'

'Worth a few bob too, I'd say.'

'Please tell mother,' Connie said as she slipped out again.

They were on their second day out of New York, and already Sarah Moore had met an old friend. Linda Davis was travelling to London with her father on a business trip. Now they were sipping tea together in the first-class tea-room. They had already discussed all their friends – who was doing what, marrying whom, travelling, fighting in the war and so on. Now they had got round to the mystery of the lifeboat drills. Both of them had travelled by liner before, and Linda Davis had crossed the Atlantic six times in all. On each trip, the pair agreed, the crews had been exercised in lifeboat drill, and these exercises had provided some entertainment for the passengers. Very little happens on board a ship on a long ocean voyage, and any small change in the daily round of breakfast, lunch, afternoon tea and dinner was something to be remembered. Linda Davis recalled one particularly entertaining occasion when the crew had dropped the lifeboat over the side and the ship had had to be stopped to pick it up again, a long-drawn-out affair in which, it was rumoured, the captain positively exploded at their mistakes.

But Sarah Moore, who had an exaggerated respect for anyone with real skill, said, 'But don't you think they're usually so skilful?'

'I quite agree,' replied Linda Davis. 'Which makes it all the more mysterious, don't you think?'

They both nodded conspiratorially.

'I guess they just haven't got round to it yet.'

'I have heard,' Sarah lowered her voice to say it, 'and the source is someone who really does know one of the officers, that with the war, all the best sailors have volunteered for the Navy. I am told Captain Turner is quite depressed by the quality of his crew. I am told he has declared he would not put out of port in peacetime if even one of them were aboard.'

Just then Oisín burst through the doors, almost knocking down a waiter carrying a huge silver tray of china cups and teapots and milk jugs, and careered across the tearoom, searching wildly for his mother. He changed direction just before a table that had two very elderly and disapproving ladies sitting at it, and came to a full stop beside his mother.

'I've just seen Connie!' he said. 'She was walking on the boat-deck with that Tom Boland, you know him.' He gasped to catch his breath. 'Guess what! She saw this famous fellow. What's-his-name. She said you would be amazed.'

'What famous fellow, child?' Sarah Moore asked. 'Catch your breath and say "How do you do?" to Miss Davis. And mind your manners. This is a tearoom, not a field.'

Oisín caught his breath in great noisy gulps, said 'How do you do?' to Miss Davis and then remembered the name of the famous fellow.

'Sir Huge Lane!' he cried delightedly. 'That's the fellow. Huge Lane. Connie said you would be amazed!'

Sarah and Linda laughed. 'Hugh,' Sarah said. 'Sir Hugh Lane. What about him?'

'He's here. On the ship. So Connie said. She actually saw him. She pointed him out to me. Mother, who is he?'

The two women laughed and Sarah said, 'Run along, Oisín, and tell Connie that I want to see her at once, there's a good boy. I'll explain all about your famous fellow later.'

Oisín was more than a little disappointed at the effect produced by his news. Connie had told it to him as if it was a state secret. 'Don't tell mother,' she had said. 'I want to tell her myself. She will be amazed.' So, naturally, he had wanted to get there first. He had run all over the ship at his top speed, which he estimated at about ten knots, and looked into all the first-class rooms, and along the promenade deck and everywhere. It was only by accident that he had tried the tearoom because it never occurred to him that anyone would want to spend such a beautiful afternoon drinking tea. To tell the truth, he was a little disappointed at his mother's attitude to the voyage. Beforehand she had been full of useful and interesting stories. The *Lusitania*, she had told him, was capable (he loved that word, 'capable') of twenty-seven knots, and a knot was one nautical mile. A nautical mile was longer than a real mile, though why, he didn't know. He guessed it was because it took longer to travel by sea, but had long ago made a mental note to ask one of the officers. Even more interestingly, his mother was able to tell him that the *Lusitania* had been built very strongly, so that in times of grave danger she could easily be converted to a warship, a light cruiser. That was the most exciting fact of all – that he was crossing the Atlantic in a light cruiser. Well, more or less a light cruiser, anyway.

But now his mother spent her time drinking tea, walking on the boat-deck, chatting to people whose names he could never remember, eating meals, dozing on the deckchairs and going to bed early. She said it was very restful. He thought it was shocking. That his mother – his mother, of all people, who was capable of arguing with a gatepost over Home Rule for Ireland, or the vote for women, who once threw a soup bowl at the head of a man who dared to suggest that the Irish would never be able to govern themselves – that his mother was behaving like . . . well, like other people's mothers. He could hardly believe it!

That was why he had gone down to the engine room. At first he told himself he was investigating. He wanted to see if the ship was carrying ammunition, as that fellow Tom Boland, that Connie was so interested in, had hinted. He hoped it was and that he would find some. He didn't intend to steal any of it, just to borrow a rifle or two for protection, in case the Germans did attack. He felt he could be quite useful if there was a battle. Then when he found himself in that huge, smoky, clattering oven of an engine room, he thought he had found heaven. The heat was stifling. The noise was unbearable. There were men everywhere going about their work in a busy, purposeful way. He simply sat down on the top step of the ladder and gazed at this unimaginably perfect scene. Why didn't anyone tell him that this wonderland was here, just a few decks down from his own cabin? He imagined all the happy hours he would be able to pass down here, chatting to the engineers and the stokers, helping out here and there, learning a bit about engines. When Father came home from the war he would be able to impress him by fixing his aeroplane engine, or getting the motor car working again.

Then he had been rudely dragged out by a stoker, hauled up like a naughty child to the first-class cabins and handed over like a parcel to old Dunphy, the steward. It was humiliating.

Now he threw himself down in a dejected mood on one of the cane chairs in the grand entrance and stared out at the glimmering sea as it went by. How was he ever going to have an adventure in the few days left at sea if he was prevented from going everywhere that was interesting on the ship? As his thoughts turned on schemes to liven the dull days, he slowly became aware that the fellow sitting in the next cane chair, just on the other side of the potted palm, calmly reading some book or other, was in fact the famous fellow that Connie had pointed out to him earlier. The Lane fellow.

Now Oisín began to wonder why he was famous. Perhaps he was a murderer, escaping from the law in America. Or perhaps he was an anarchist who had thrown a bomb at the President, or was travelling to Europe to throw a bomb at the Tsar of Russia. Or perhaps he was a spy. Or a famous explorer. Or a fellow who had been in the Olympic Games. Oisín was now so curious that he simply had to find out. He gathered his courage, took a deep breath, turned towards the potted palm, and said in a very grown-up voice, 'I say, aren't you the famous fellow, Sir Lane?'

Hugh Lane looked about to see where the voice was coming from. He realised that it was coming from very low down near the base of the potted palm and leant forward to see who the speaker might be. He was surprised to see that it was a very small boy in a tweed jacket and short trousers, his socks down around his ankles.

'Hello,' he said. 'Did you speak?'

'I was asking if you're Sir Lane, the famous fellow?'

Hugh Lane chuckled. 'That's me,' he said. 'Hugh Lane.' He held out his hand and Oisín grasped it. He felt more than a little amazed that here he was actually shaking the hand of the famous man that Connie had been so excited about. 'You can call me Hugh if you like. All my friends do.'

'Mine's Oisín,' Oisín said. 'I'm supposed to be called after a poem by someone or other. I always have to explain that or else everyone says, "Oisín, how do you spell that?" or else, "What does it mean?"'

'Very annoying.'

'Awful. And sometimes I'm not so good at spelling.'

'Neither am I,' Hugh Lane told him. 'Most adults only pretend to be good at it.'

'Golly!' Oisín had started to say 'golly' in Boston. He had heard several people say it and quite liked the sound of the word. 'Do you mind if I ask you something?'

'Not in the least.'

'What I want to know is this. You see, I know you're famous, because my sister Connie pointed you out. But I don't know *why* you're famous. And how famous are you if I haven't heard about you?'

Hugh Lane chuckled again. He was a tall, thin, rather handsome man, with a large moustache and clear, warm eyes. Oisín rather liked him. 'That depends, really,' he said. 'If I tell you what I do, will you promise to keep it a complete secret?'

'Of course,' Oisín said at once.

'Well, I buy and sell art. Paintings and such things. At this very moment, in a lead-lined box deep in the hold of this ship, there are several paintings by the most famous artists who ever put brush to canvas. Rubens, for example, and Titian. I am taking them to Ireland because I wish Ireland to have the greatest collection of art the world has ever seen. One day, when we are a free country, we will be famous for our art and literature.'

Oisín blinked in awe. At first, when he heard that the famous man was only a buyer of pictures, he had been disappointed. But now the idea of the lead-lined box full of fabulously expensive paintings had taken hold of his imagination. Here was adventure indeed. What if an art thief had followed Sir Hugh aboard? What if enemies of Ireland were plotting to prevent Sir Hugh bringing the paintings there? He silently pledged himself to the defence of Sir Hugh and his lead-lined box. His father would approve, he knew. After all, he was doing it for Ireland.

'Now, young chap, I must go. Perhaps we could talk again some day. Or perhaps we will meet at home in Ireland.'

They stood up and Oisín shook hands gravely with the famous man.

'Goodbye,' Sir Hugh said.

'Goodbye, sir,' Oisín replied. 'Thank you for telling me about your paintings. I shall keep your secret, never fear.' He stood in the grand entrance, watching the tall, thin man move out into the sunlight. Beyond him the deep blue sea stretched for a thousand miles in every direction, giving no indication of its power to create and destroy, nor of the fate that lay in store for the famous man and the curious boy.

THURSDAY 4 MAY 1915

A GHOST FROM THE PAST

The cry of "Sail ho! Starboard bow!' caused chuckles up and down the passageways of the submarine. Good old Gunther Rueff was at it again. What a joker! But Walter Schwieger didn't see it as funny at all. They were off the west coast of Ireland now, and for two days they had been chasing imaginary ships that turned out to be clouds, and real ships that turned out to be too fast. He was on edge and irritable. This time, he vowed, he would discipline Rueff. It was all very well having a joker on board. It made for a better crew, and he had to hand it to Rueff, he could make everyone laugh. But sometimes he went too far. He would have to learn.

He dragged himself up the ladder to the conning tower and was annoyed to find Otto Lanz already up there, chuckling quietly and slapping Rueff on the back.

'I have had enough of your jokes, Rueff,' Walter Schwieger told him. 'This is no laughing matter! You will report to me at . . . ' Then he, too, saw the sails, low down on the horizon but quite clear, a schooner, close-hauled and headed towards them. She was too far away to have seen them. A few seabirds, puffins perhaps, wallowed in the swell close by on the starboard side. Apart from the sailing ship and the birds and the U-boat the sea appeared to be empty of life.

'Down, everyone!' Walter Schwieger shouted. 'We will dive.'

Gunther Rueff disappeared down through the hatch, shouting, 'Alarm! Alarm! Dive!'

Otto Lanz looked at him in shock. 'But, *Herr Ober-leutnant*, that is only a sailing ship.'

'Otto,' Walter Schwieger said severely, 'you should know not to ask questions. That is an enemy vessel. Our duty is to sink enemy vessels. That is all there is to be said.'

'I apologise,' Otto Lanz replied, clicking his heels together in the Prussian fashion and standing very straight. There was resentment in his posture and his eyes were fixed on the badge in Walter Schwieger's cap.

'Go on, Otto,' Walter Schwieger told him gently. 'Get below and plot the course.'

He stayed in the conning tower a few moments longer, watching a ghost from the days of sail work up to windward. He reflected that once upon a time he would have been captain of such a vessel himself, trimming sails and rubbing his hands together in delight at the thought of a fat prize. He would have anticipated a straight fight, out in the open, cannons blazing. The best ship and the best captain would win. Instead he was slinking below the waves, laying a cowardly trap for a ship that could neither escape him nor fight back.

An hour later he and Otto Lanz were taking turns to gaze through the periscope at the *Earl of Latham*, a battered old schooner of about 150 tons. She was close enough for them to be able to read her name. Under tattered grey sails, she was making slow progress in light winds. *U-20*'s crew were in good humour, thinking that the sinking of a rotten old schooner was good sport, almost a joke. Most of them thought of such ships as laughable, old-fashioned things, such as their parents boasted about. Sinking one would be something new, something different, a break in the monotony of the voyage. And Walter Schwieger had to admit that the atmosphere on board *U-20* was much better now. The crew had lost their gloomy looks. One old salt, the oldest member of the crew, began to sing an old song from his youth when he was sailor on a full-rigged ship out of Hamburg. The crew joined in, thirty deep male voices, a little husky from the bad air, and Walter Schwieger let them sing because the singing would be good for them. He did not need silence to think. If he did he would have made a very bad submarine commander. Besides, the sound was impressive in that tin-can hull.

'What do you think, Otto?'

'Not worth a torpedo,' Lanz replied.

'Do you think she might be armed?' The British often used innocent-looking merchant ships to lure submarines to the surface. Once the submarine was a clear shot, false walls would drop away, or a gun would peep out from behind bales of hay that should have been for feeding cattle. Q-ships, they were called. They roamed the seaways, waiting for a submarine to find them – boats that weren't worth wasting a valuable torpedo on. Walter Schwieger knew that several U-boats had been sunk that way.

'I cannot see where they could hide guns, *Herr Ober-leutnant*,' Otto Lanz said. 'But perhaps there is some way.' He looked quizzically at his captain. There was a change in Otto Lanz's behaviour and attitude that Walter Schwieger could not put his finger on.

He thought for a moment and then said, 'Blow the ballast tanks. We will attack her on the surface. Gun crew to attend their stations. Stand by.'

On board the *Earl of Latham*, it was the first mate who saw the dark-grey shape of *U-20* emerging from the Atlantic swell. He shouted for the captain to come on deck, and thought wildly that if he could tack the ship quickly he might just be able to escape. Then he realised that in these light winds even a very slow submarine would be able to overtake them. He shrugged his shoulders and stuck his hands firmly into his reefer-jacket pockets to await events.

The captain, when he did come on deck, had very little else to suggest. He and the mate walked aft to the sorry excuse for a quarterdeck and stood near the wheel. They gazed bleakly at the menacing U-boat.

Walter Schwieger hailed them through his loudspeaker and ordered that they heave to. It was the old order that had been passed from ship to ship for centuries. Heave to. The captain ordered all sails furled. By then a gun crew was standing at the submarine's deck gun. *U-20* approached quite close and Walter Schwieger informed the captain that he intended to sink them.

'You'd hardly think she were worth it,' the mate said.

'Aye,' the captain replied. 'Rotten old tub. They're welcome to 'er.'

'Order your crew to abandon ship,' Walter Schwieger repeated in clear English, a slight trace of an accent betraying his nationality. 'You have ten minutes.'

The captain was grateful for the time. He organised his lifeboats, stocking them well, made sure that all the crew had extra clothes, roused out two bottles of brandy against the cold and took his logbook and charts, compasses and sextant. By the time he was climbing down the side everything was in order. He took one last look at the *Earl of Latham*. There was little love in the look. She was a cranky old tub that leaked at every seam, that was rotten in the bilge as far as the third strake, riddled with teredo worm, and ironsick, so that you never knew if a bolt or a nail would be firm or come away in your hand. If the submarine had not offered to sink her, she would have been a watery grave for her crew sooner or later. Still, the captain had the strange feeling that here was the end of something, the last day of some great adventure that had gone on for hundreds of years. It was as if the *Earl of Latham* was the last sailing ship, and that submarine over there, covering and uncovering in the eternal Atlantic swell, was the future. If so, it was a future that the captain wanted no part of. If he reached shore alive, he would never go to sea again.

'Give way there,' he called to the oarsmen. They pulled hard, anxious to get clear of the schooner before the shooting started, having heard stories of German submarines killing men in lifeboats. As they pulled past the submarine, Walter Schwieger saluted them. Then, as an afterthought, he called across to them that if they required anything he would try to find it.

The captain shook his head and thanked him, saying they were well provided for and the coast was not very far away. He raised a hand and pointed eastwards, where a faint blue line showed itself – the coast of County Clare, a dangerous shore with uncertain harbours. A chart open on his lap showed the captain the yawning mouth of the Shannon estuary and the little harbour of Carrigaholt, a safe place, he knew, having sheltered there many a time before. He hoped good old Mrs O'Shea still kept the pub there. She would serve him up a hot whiskey punch. They knew how to treat shipwrecked sailors in County Clare!

Walter Schwieger saluted again and wished them a safe return as they pulled away from him, their oars dipping and flashing in the sunshine. Then he turned his attention to the gunnery. Gunther Rueff was in charge, the best gunlayer they had, and Walter Schwieger was anxious that no shot should go wild. He need not have worried. Four shells, one after the other, pounded into the wooden hull. One went straight through and exploded in the sea on the other side. Soon she was burning and, at the same time, settling slowly into the water. Walter Schwieger ordered the cease-fire and the gun crew closed down the gun and stopped its barrel so that it would remain dry underwater. Then he and Otto Lanz watched the old ship slowly slip beneath the surface, flames climbing upwards through the sails, masts and spars like sailors struggling to remain above the water. She went down by the stern, and as her bowsprit pointed high into the sky, they saw a horde of brown rats rushing up it, climbing out to the very tip, pushing and jostling each other as the water rose, some falling off and swimming frantically away, others squealing and biting until the last inch of wood was gone.

'What a sad sight,' Otto Lanz said. 'It reminds me of the stories of ancient Greece. The burning of ships was a terrible thing to the seafarers of that time.'

'I trained in a sailing ship, did I tell you that?'

'No, *Herr Oberleutnant.* You did not.'

'Oh yes. A full-rigged ship. The Imperial Navy believed it was good for her seamen to understand the old ways. But I never thought I would sink one myself. I, too, find it terribly sad.'

'It is part of some old heroic way of life, yes?' There was an eager light in Lanz's eyes. Whenever he talked about his books – the ancient warriors of Troy or Greece, the distant battles of Agamemnon, Achilles and Hector – his face shone and his eyes gleamed.

'That's it exactly. A heroic way of life. Those old sailors were heroes indeed. But we . . . we fight a dirty war, approaching in secrecy, using cunning and double-dealing to win our fights. At best the enemy never see us. We send our deadly arrows into their bellies and they never know who loosed them. At worst they chase and kill us, and then we go to the bottom unknown. They never know what they have done.' Walter Schwieger shook his head. 'There are no heroes in the submarine service, Otto. Just good crews and easy targets.'

By now the *Earl of Latham* was gone and the sea was littered with debris: spars, oars, broken timber and, of course, the rats. One or two had actually climbed onto the floating planks and were crouched there, balefully watching their comrades, who were now beginning to swim in an organised fashion towards the submarine. To the east, the lifeboats were still in sight, moving steadily over a glassy sea. Walter Schwieger gave the order to get under way and the U-boat began to move. Soon the rats were left behind. How many of them would eventually swim ashore in Ireland? Very few, if any. Yet the rat was a great survivor.

Otto Lanz went below to devise a new course that would take them to the south coast of Ireland. There they would cruise up and down past Cork and Kinsale, where ships kept close in to the shore, checking their navigation against the lights and seamarks, and hoping that the Western Approaches Fleet would pick them up and convoy them safely home. The sea lanes there were almost as obvious as country roads. *U-20* would have no trouble finding targets.

But Walter Schwieger remained in the tower, even after two sailors came on watch, stamping round to keep their feet warm and staring through Zeiss binoculars. Walter Schwieger was thinking about what he had said to Otto Lanz, about how the war he was fighting was a dirty one, and he was also thinking about his orders. 'Sink all merchant shipping,' he was told, 'even passenger ships. They are legitimate targets.' In February his government had declared 'unrestricted submarine warfare' and had been sinking anything that came within the war zone around Britain and Ireland. Unable to defeat the British in the trenches of the Western Front, the government hoped to starve them into submission by preventing supplies from reaching English ports. So far, the sub-marine war had been devastating. Walter Schwieger, like most U-boat commanders, believed such ships to be fair game, although he always hoped to see the crew escape in lifeboats. But sooner or later, he knew, he would be faced with some passenger steamer full of civilians, and his orders were quite clear. 'Sink any merchant vessel on sight.' He was not even required to give a warning. The thought of that filled him with dread.

Three hours later they were off the Kerry coast. An aircraft had been reported shortly after the sinking of the *Earl of Latham*, and although he did not think it likely that one could be so far offshore, still he had no desire to take chances. If an aircraft did spot him, it might decide to drop a bomb. Such a thing had happened, he knew. At the very least it would report his presence to the British Admiralty and then he would have the sub-marine-chasers to contend with. Just in case, he had ordered *U-20* submerged. Since then, they had been running below the surface. The batteries were running down and the air was foul with the smell of urine and sweat and bilge water. It was hard to breathe, and his eyes watered constantly. The U-boat's walls dripped like the inside of a cave. Every instrument was clouded with water droplets, and the rags with which they wiped them were themselves wet through. Walter Schwieger's clothes felt like he had been swimming in them.

'We will surface, I think, Otto, yes? It is time. We will all choke in our own smell unless we do.' He smiled at his little joke. 'Up periscope. Let us see what is on top.' But Otto Lanz did not smile. There had been a coolness between them since Walter Schwieger had rebuked him on the bridge of the conning tower. Otto Lanz did not like to think of himself as fighting a dirty war. He needed to think in terms of knights and warriors crusading for goodness. For him, the submarine service was indeed heroic, the men who manned the U-boats were the direct descendants of the great warriors of ancient times, who pitted themselves against impossible odds. And in truth, Walter Schwieger thought, the odds were against them. Who would choose to live half their days thirty feet or three hundred feet below the surface? No ancient hero endured the appalling conditions that submariners did, living together in an enormous sausage filled with cans of food, high explosives, battery acid, diesel oil and human beings! And what would their end be if they were detected? An oil slick on the surface meant a submarine had been attacked successfully. Destroyer captains would report that slick with satisfaction. It was almost like killing a mad dog.

Walter Schwieger realised that something was hardening around his own heart too. He no longer worried about whether Otto or the men were happy. He thought now of Lanz's bitterness and it did not touch him. Let him be angry. Let him feel hurt. He was a man like any other. This ship was a fighting machine. It too had a duty. Walter Schwieger was the brain, the part of the mechanism that made the machine work. Otto Lanz, the pilot, merely directed the wheels. He could navigate just as well angry as happy. One day they would do something terrible, something appalling, and the hardness of his heart would stand him in good stead then. Others had already done such things. Everyone knew the stories from the Western Front – the bayoneting of prisoners, the gas, the shooting of deserters and malingerers. This was the most terrible war. There never was or never would be so terrible a thing again. He, Walter Schwieger, was merely a small part of the terror.

He bent to the eyepiece and swivelled slowly, checking the horizon for signs of smoke, or breaking water that might indicate a destroyer or fast cruiser. Suddenly he was looking straight at a grey wall.

'A ship! My God!'

'What?' Otto Lanz half-shouted, if anything even more astonished than his captain. 'What ship? What description?'

'I can't tell. She's too close. Prepare to fire a torpedo!'

The torpedo drill began, Lanz waiting in a fever of excitement, pencil in hand, ready to do the calculations. To successfully direct a torpedo over the sea at a moving target, it was necessary to calculate the speed of the target and set it against the speed of the torpedo. The range had to be worked out and included in the sum. It was tricky thing to do, and more often than not the firing solution was wrong and the torpedo missed. If they were very lucky they might get a second shot. But there was no chance for calculation this time.

'*Los!*'

The hull shuddered slightly as the torpedo left its tube. Through the periscope Walter Schwieger followed the bubble-track towards the ship, the white chalk-line of the equation of death. At the same time he began to see things on her deck. The captain walking up and down, a small whistle in his mouth, the crew cleaning the decks forward. Then he noticed rows and rows of wooden partitions all along the decks, and between the partitions the shining backs of horses.

'Oh God!' he said. 'Horses. The ship is full of horses.' Otto Lanz gasped.

At that moment Walter Schwieger saw the ship's captain turn and see the line of the torpedo streaking through the Atlantic towards him. What would he do? It was too late for him to order the ship to change course. The torpedo was too fast. Would he run to the other side, hoping to avoid the explosion? Shout a warning and begin launching boats?

The captain threw his hands over his face and stood waiting for the explosion.

The chalkline ended at the ship's sides. A column of water erupted, two hundred metres high and fifty broad, and the submarine shuddered. The crew were thrown from side to side. Walter Schwieger, even though he had been expecting it, was jolted backwards so that a seaman had to catch him, or he would have been knocked unconscious by the piping that ran everywhere.

He was up in an instant, eyes pressed to the periscope again.

'Hit abaft the second funnel!' he shouted. 'She'll go down on that one.' There were sailors everywhere now, swarming to the lifeboats, desperately manhandling the falls to let them down into the sea, black-faced stokers and officers and grooms belonging to the horses. Some of them were fighting for places. Others were struggling to put on life jackets. The captain was gone from the deck. Could he have been blown into the sea by the blast? Unlikely. Perhaps he had gone below for his compass.

On board *U-20* they all heard the second explosion and knew what it was.

'A boiler!' Gunther Rueff hissed. 'The boiler has blown.'

Cold seawater flooding inwards had met the ship's boilers. They were white-hot, driving steam into the pistons to make the ship move. When the cold water and the hot boiler met, the boiler blew, as devastatingly as if it were packed with high explosive. It broke the ship's back.

Through the periscope Walter Schwieger could see that the decks were hidden by clouds of scalding hot steam. The horses, maddened by it, had kicked their way out of their flimsy wooden stables and were bucking and rearing among the blinded seamen. He saw one black mare leap out and down and land in the middle of a half-full lifeboat. Boat and mare and men disappeared in a little explosion of matchwood and water.

'Dear God!' Walter Schwieger said. 'Dear God, what a sight!'

He straightened up and gestured for the 'scope to be lowered. They were all looking at him. An appalled silence had settled on them. Not a man moved or whispered. There were no cheers or hand-shaking, such as often happened after a success. But, magnified by the sea and the sounding-board of the hull, they heard the groaning and creaking of the dying ship, and they could take no joy in it.

Friday 5 May 1915

A Dinner Party

Connie had hoped to be able to see the sunset with Tom Boland. On the previous evening, they had stood on the forward end of the boat-deck for an hour, first waiting for the sun to sink to the horizon, then watching it go down in a blaze of glory, and finally gazing with awe at the magnificent dying of the light. They had talked of Ireland and their homes, their families, their friends. At one point they had thought about the future, and Connie felt there was a magic in the wind. It seemed to be *their* future, not just a thing that they would travel into together, but somehow a shared thing, a future between them. And Tom was not at all like the other boys she knew. They were only interested in horses and cricket. They sounded just like their fathers, and she expected they would grow up into huntin', shootin' and fishin' people with loud, jocular voices and fingers like small parsnips. As far as they were concerned, girls were things that you sometimes met around the house, but that rarely ventured into the open air, delicate things that couldn't hold a gun properly and had to sit sideways on a horse.

She hated that attitude. Tom understood that she would not settle for the things a woman of her class was expected to want – ordering the servants, managing the household finances, devising menus for parties. She would not be domesticated. Tom understood all that.

'Of course,' he said, as if it was all perfectly reasonable, and need not even be mentioned, 'that's all gone anyhow.' He swept his hand across the visible horizon. 'The war knocked the stuffing out of that. Look at the girls working in factories in England. Married women. Their husbands are at the front. Don't think they'll go back to the house like sheep going through a gate when it's all over. Listen, Connie, the world will never be the same again.' He said it with such calm assurance that it seemed to be a certainty. Standing by his side, Connie had never felt so confident that her dreams would be fulfilled, that all her hopes were not mere hopes but possibilities.

'Oh Tom,' she said, 'I really do believe it will happen. You make it sound easy!'

'Indeed it is,' he told her. 'All we have to do is want it.'

Tom was two years older than her and seemed much wiser. He was going home to Ireland to begin cramming for his matriculation examination. In a year or two he would be at university. Connie was beginning to think she would like to go there herself.

'Do you know,' she said, 'I don't ever want to have servants! I think being a servant is a hateful thing!'

Tom laughed. 'But some servants have much better lives than if they had stayed at home. Their homes are so pitiful. Have you ever been to Dublin? Did you walk in the Liberties? Have you seen the homes of the small cottiers and spalpeens that are all over the countryside? Wouldn't they be better off living in the attic of your house? Cooking in the warm kitchens? Eating the left-overs?'

Connie was annoyed at that. 'Our May does not eat the leftovers. She's one of the family! And we only have one other house servant, and she comes from a very fine house and goes home every evening.'

Tom had a very low opinion of the way the landed gentry treated those who worked for them, but Connie's family were not rich and did much of their own work themselves, whereas Tom's family had lots of servants and lived in a big house on St Stephen's Green in Dublin. They had quarrelled once already, shortly after they met on their second day out, over what Tom called her 'principles'. He said she didn't just want the world to be different; she wanted to turn it upside down. She said she certainly did, and the sooner the better. Then he had made her laugh by calling her 'a bit of an anarchist', and that was the end of the quarrel.

But they hadn't quarrelled that evening. The glory of the sunset and the rising moon had ensured that. Better still, when the sun was gone and the air grew chill, Tom Boland had taken off his jacket and draped it across her shoulders, and for one glorious instant she had felt the warm solidity of his shoulders. She knew she was in love.

That was why this invitation – 'summons' would be a better word – to dine with mother and her stuffy friends was so unwelcome. Usually the young people dined first and had the evening to themselves. Adults could congregate in the great dining room with its huge dome and fish-faced waiters! The young did not have to suffer the boredom of adult 'wit' and conversation. Connie's mother was all right, but she usually succumbed on these occasions to the same level of intelligence as those she was sitting beside. Connie rarely saw her sharp brain at work, and there was never a good argument really.

'Never mind,' Tom told her. 'I've offered to dine with my pater anyway. He was pleased about that, because he says I've been avoiding him.' They smiled at each other in complicity. 'I'll be only a table away. I'll be fairly close.' Tom always called his father 'pater'. Latin was such a distinguished language. 'Our table'll be quite near yours.'

'Will you wink at me once in a while, Tom? It would make it all bearable.'

'I will, surely! I'll give you the occasional sly wink. No one will notice at all. And you can wink back.' Tom was always winking. Whenever he had something funny to say he gave her a huge wink, as big as a shade coming down on a window. Connie had not yet mastered the skill, so they had practised for a time, Tom demonstrating the whole range, and they had laughed and laughed.

'Why don't you sit by me, dear?' Linda Davis said, when Connie came to the table. It was meant kindly, Connie knew. Otherwise she would have to sit beside the fat Englishwoman with the terrifying glass eye.

'Thank you, Mrs Davis.'

'Well, well, this must be Constance,' a very elderly man said. Connie knew he was Lord Somebody-or-other and Tom called him 'Lord Muck'. Mother disliked him intensely. 'How do you do, my dear?' He stood and shook Connie's hand, and held a chair for Sarah Moore. 'Ain't it delightful to have young people?'

The officer she had met on the first day was there, slightly too far away to talk to. She smiled at him and he waved his hand at her. Mrs Hodnett was there too, a middle-aged woman from Cork, an acquaintance of Mother's. There was the fat Englishwoman whom Tom and Connie privately nicknamed 'Old Glassy Eye' and an even more terrifying man that had hairy hands, enormous sideburns and skin that seemed to have the same dead appearance as a bat's. They called him 'Batface'. An American completed the company. They knew he was American because they had heard him say so. He seemed a pleasant sort of fellow.

The food was Cunard's best effort in this time of war, and very good because it had been taken on in America. On the journey back from England it would not be so good.

Connie started with *paté de foie gras* on fine slivers of toast. The sea air had made her ravenously hungry and she felt she had been eating since the moment they left the Fourteenth Street pier! She followed this with perch, baked *à la meunière*. She was so concentrated on the food in front of her that she didn't notice a distinct frostiness creeping into the conversation, an edgy atmosphere. Had she been paying more attention, she would have heard the warning signs and might have steered her mother out of it. She had done it before. It was over the main course of roast beef that this frostiness heated up into a full-scale row. It was Linda Davis who had, in all innocence, led the way with something about the third-class passengers. The officer, whose name, Connie now remembered, was Patrick Regan, had said, 'Would you be surprised to hear that the third-class passenger list is only one-third full?'

Linda Davis said that she found it rather surprising, considering the high standards that Cunard prided themselves on, the food even in third class being considered so good, and the accommodation clean and comfortable. Perhaps, she suggested, the German advertisement warning passengers not to travel to the war zone had frightened many of them away.

At that point Batface had made a remark about 'shameless cowardice', and the officer had changed the subject, not wanting, everyone assumed, to allow the subject of torpedoes to come up.

But Batface wasn't about to be put off. He drank a full glass of wine in one huge gulp, a hairy hand locked onto the fragile stem of the glass, and announced in a loud voice that he believed the common man would never show courage unless he were driven to it by an officer with a revolver. He gave it as a fact and said that he had seen it himself in the Crimea. 'Cowards! Cowardly malingerers who never do their duty unless it is under the threat of court martial! That is the common man.'

'I say,' Lord Muck put in, 'that's a bit much, old chap. I mean to say, what about the Hearts of Oak? What about the good old Tommy? Sound chaps, every one. Noble, even.'

Batface snorted contemptuously into his newly filled wineglass. 'Permit me to laugh, my lord,' he said. 'I take it you have not seen service yourself?'

Lord Muck looked suddenly bored. He fiddled with a ring on his right hand and gazed pointedly at another table.

At that moment Tom's family came in and made their way to the table opposite and Connie was distracted. She was struck again by how handsome Tom looked, particularly in that dark dinner jacket and the wing collar. He looked quite grown up; no one would guess he was only two years older than her. There was Tom's father – something to do with banking, Tom said, though he wasn't quite certain what his father's business interests were – and Tom's mother, who had been unwell with seasickness for the entire voyage. As he passed, Tom gave her one of his 'secret winks', so broad and obvious that it distorted his entire face and made him look like a toby jug. She almost laughed aloud. He sat down on the far side of the table and seemed more intent on studying her than his menu card.

'Of course,' Batface said, 'it's all due to these trade-union johnnies. These fellows are ruining the country. They will make us lose the war if we don't tackle them. Defeat, that's what those bounders want. And victory for Kaiser Bill!'

So far, it had been predictable enough. Connie saw that her mother was pale with anger, but restraining herself. Sarah Moore couldn't abide people like Batface. Besides, her sympathies were definitely with the 'trade-union johnnies'. However, Batface would eventually run out of nasty things to say, and the embarrassment he was causing would evaporate. The conversation would turn to food, or the weather, and everything would go back to normal.

But it was not to happen. The American seemed to be chewing over Batface's last comment. Something was bothering him about it, though he had not said ten words since the meal began.

Now he came out with the remark that started the whole thing boiling. 'I guess,' he said, in a slow drawl, 'that it would be pointless to tell you that you don't know what you're talking about. I guess it would be pointless to say you should not speak about things you can't understand. I guess that would be beyond you, sir.'

A shocked silence descended on the table. Connie saw her mother sit up straight and look at her fellow American with interest. Connie knew that look. She suspected an ally.

'I don't believe we've been introduced, sir,' Sarah Moore said. 'I believe we are compatriots. My name is Sarah Moore.'

'Michael Hargreaves,' the American said. 'Delighted to make your acquaintance.'

Batface watched the introductions with malevolent intent. Connie could see his brain working overtime.

'Americans, of course,' he said, and looked around at the others, as though to confirm that they understood the appalling nature of that statement.

'Indeed we are,' Sarah Moore said. 'I was born and raised in Boston, Mr Hargreaves, though I married an Irishman and have lived in Ireland for nearly twenty years. By your accent I take it you are a New Englander?'

Batface, who had been spluttering and making faces at his roast beef, said, 'And I take it, sir, that you are a foreigner on a British ship and would do well to be polite!'

He said it in the same triumphant voice with which he would have delivered a crushing insult. 'A foreigner and a coward, no doubt.'

There was a gasp around the table.

'Steady on,' Patrick Regan said, as though he were addressing a nervous sailor.

The American turned slowly towards Batface. 'I have not had the honour of being introduced to you, I'm glad to say,' he said. 'That being the case, I can hardly speak to you. I am addressing this lady here at present, and I would be obliged if you stopped talking.'

Now Lord Muck intervened. 'Quite right. Quite right. This is a dinner after all, what? Spoil our digestions completely. Discussion over dinner quite ruins the digestion.'

Mrs Hodnett agreed. 'In Ireland, we bar politics at the dining table,' she added.

'Very wise, ma'am,' Lord Muck said. 'I compliment you on it.' Mrs Hodnett blushed deeply and looked down at her plate, where a mixture of brown gravy, greasy peas and blood from the underdone beef had cooled into a kind of stagnant pond.

But Old Glassy Eye had been glaring down at them through her one working pupil. The mention of Ireland seemed to cause a change in her, as if some pent-up force had been released. Her breath seemed to pop out of her, followed by what sounded like a snarl.

'You live in Ireland?' she asked. The question seemed innocent enough, if you had not watched her previous reactions. Mrs Hodnett nodded her head and prepared to launch into a glowing description of Ireland in summer –

fuchsia blooming in the hedgerows, the bright yellow furze, the ripening apples. But before she could get off her mark, Old Glassy Eye had opened fire.

'I do hope you are not one of those Home Rulers. Dreadful people. Quite the nasty animal they are. Biting the hand that fed them. They are so ungrateful. After all, the British Empire has had a civilising effect wherever it has gone. Look at India. Ireland, I may say, has had more need of civilisation than even India. You are not one of those Home Rulers, are you?'

Mrs Hodnett was thrown into complete confusion by the suggestion. Certainly she was not a Home Ruler. The very thought. And in this time of need when the wolf, as it were, was at the door, in the shape of the Hun, who were dropping actual bombs on London. Perish the thought.

'Jolly glad to hear you say so, ma'am. It ain't often you hear the Irish say such things,' Lord Muck said. He beamed down at her. 'The sentiment does you credit. I compliment you on it.'

But Connie was watching her mother. She saw the telltale signs of an explosion coming: the white face, the gleaming eyes, the lips already moving to frame some astonishing statement. Across the way, Tom Boland was making sympathetic faces at her. He clearly thought that she was suffering the pangs of boredom. In fact, Connie was beginning to enjoy herself. She foresaw a most frightful row. The adults would be at each other's throats in a moment. How Oisín, tucked away in his sleeping cabin, would wish to be here, if he only knew! They would all be lucky if the captain did not call out the master-at-arms and have them clapped in irons!

'I take it, ma'am,' Sarah Moore said, not looking at Old Glassy Eye at all, but staring steadily at her own wine-glass, 'that you lost your eye in the service of your country.' It was a bombshell of an insult, better than anything Batface could have come up with.

A stunned silence settled on the table for the second time. This was going too far. But Connie knew that when her mother got going, it was unrestricted warfare.

'Losing an eye in the service of one's country is such a noble thing,' Sarah Moore went on. 'After all, Admiral Nelson had only one eye. And of course, Queen Elizabeth had only one tooth, more or less, but that is an entirely different matter. There is a long tradition of one-eyed people in the British Empire. It accounts for the fact that Britain has never been able to see properly what she is doing. She has blundered around the world, civilising her betters and reducing them to the condition of beggars in their own countries. Such has been the experience of Ireland, I guess. Famine, of course, has a habit of making people awkward – cussed, as we say in the ex-colony of Massachusetts. And, though no doubt with one eye you could not have seen it, Ireland had a famine in which Britain permitted her to lose a few million human beings.'

Connie noticed the American staring in amazement at her mother. Suddenly he said, under his breath, 'Bravo!'

Old Glassy Eye had placed one hand over her mouth. Her good eye was rambling to left and right while her glass eye seemed to stare relentlessly at Connie. The silence was so profound that Connie was able to hear the conversation at Tom's table. Mrs Boland was talking about her seasickness, while Mr Boland was tucking into a mutton chop.

Lord Muck attempted to come to the rescue of the drowning conversation. 'I say, has anyone seen the tremendously tall chap in third class? Must be eight feet tall. A giant. What a pugilist he would make!' But no one took up the offer of rescue. Batface was on the point of going on the offensive again when Mrs Hodnett got there first.

'My dear Mrs Moore, you sound like a perfect revolutionary. If I didn't know you were of the landed gentry, I should say you were serious.'

'I am serious,' Sarah Moore said. 'I am sick and tired of British Empire this and British Empire that. If the British Empire is so great, why doesn't it win the war and let the young men come home!' Connie could see that her mother's mood had changed. With the mention of the young men, she was suddenly close to tears. There was a catch in her voice. Connie knew she was thinking of Father, and Peter Carey, and Georgie Hennessy, and young Denis Hegarty, who was only sixteen when he joined. They had all marched away with the Munster Fusiliers, Denis singing as he always did, and already Peter was dead and Georgie had lost a leg.

'Cowards! Pacifists! Rebels! Traitors!' Batface cried. He said it in a high-pitched squeak and bounced in his seat as he spoke. 'That's the Irish!'

'You haven't the slightest idea what you are saying,' Sarah Moore said. 'I do believe you haven't a brain in your head.'

Batface spluttered something about 'insufferable women'. Patrick Regan stood up suddenly and placed his napkin on the table, then sat down again just as suddenly.

The American coughed, and sipped his wine. Tom Boland gave Connie an enormous wink and a smile. Old Glassy Eye slammed her knife and fork down onto the table. A hush was descending on the nearby tables. People were beginning to notice, and pass remarks from behind their napkins.

'Of course,' Sarah Moore added, 'when we women are in government, we will abolish war. All disputes will be settled by negotiation. There will be no Empire.'

The notion of 'women in government' was an even greater shock to those seated around the table than Home Rule had been. Lord Muck was positively stunned. His mouth opened and closed soundlessly four or five times. Batface laughed bitterly, then swallowed another whole glass of wine in one gulp. Mrs Hodnett blushed.

Suddenly, Linda Davis, who had said very little until now, broke in on the sense of shock. 'Well, you have to admit that after several thousand years of masculine rule, the world is in a rather unhappy state. If the Prime Minister of England and the Chancellor of Germany had been women they would never have declared war.'

Connie knew that Linda Davis did not share her friend's radical views. Most likely she had seen that Sarah Moore's emotions were tightly strung, and had come in on her side. The effect, however, was to enrage the others. They had been angered by the idea of trade unions, by Home Rule, by criticism of the Empire, but the idea of Mr Lloyd George, the Prime Minister, changed by some horrid magic trick into a woman was the last straw. A clamour of voices now drowned out Mrs Davis's last words.

Mrs Hodnett: 'Scandalous!'

Lord Muck: 'Gad, I can hardly believe it!'

Batface: ' ... Captain should clap them in irons ... !'

Finally, Old Glassy Eye, bringing up the rear but really anxious to lead the charge, declared, 'I shall not sit here to have my King and country insulted. It will be a sad day for England if it is ever ruled by a woman. Especially,' she said, pointing a bony finger at Sarah Moore and Linda Davis, 'especially by women such as you!' She pushed her chair back, flung her linen napkin down into her roast beef and marched out of the dining room. Lord Muck, clearly of the view that he could not be seen to be shirking his duty, yet reluctant to leave the beef, rose slowly and nodded to Batface.

An extraordinary change had come over that man's face. Instead of the grey dead-bat colour, it was now a deep, lustrous purple, the colour of a heather-covered hillside in October. His hands fluttered like nervous birds from cutlery to plate and back again. His mouth worked as though he had something to say, but nothing came out. At last, standing and pulling the corners of his napkin as though to tear them, he said, 'I have heard enough now. I have been seated with madwomen. Who organised the seating for this table? I declare, it has been too much. I shall complain to the captain. Good God, what an ordeal!'

When he was gone, Lieutenant Patrick Regan let out a sigh of relief, then grinned boyishly at Connie. 'I can't say but they were asking for it,' he said. 'Though I'll catch it when he goes to the captain. Old Turner will roast me for allowing the passengers to upset themselves.'

'Poor boy,' Mrs Davis said. 'We will defend you.'

'Cowards to the end,' the American said, 'we will

probably hide, and let you take it in the neck for us!'

Connie was amazed. With the departure of the others the table had taken on a party atmosphere. Everyone seemed to have relaxed. Linda Davis was tucking into her Yorkshire pudding with relish. Sarah Moore had speared a piece of pink roast beef and was holding it high in the air like an Indian brave holding the scalp of a dead enemy. Patrick Regan was mopping his forehead with his napkin and grinning broadly.

'Sarah, don't ask me to repeat what I said,' Linda Davis said. 'I don't believe a word of it. I only said it because of you.'

'Thank you, my dear,' Sarah Moore said. 'You saved the day. I should rather be attacked by a submarine than face that one-eyed old hag again.'

'I thought you were doing pretty well,' the American said. 'You should come to Harvard. You could lecture us on Irish history. No one would dare ask you a question.'

They all laughed.

'Are you a Harvard man?' Linda Davis asked.

'Guilty, I'm afraid,' the American said. They all smiled. 'Classics, too, and that's the worst of all. I'm a Latin scholar. I'm hoping to study at the British Museum.'

'If the Germans don't get it first,' Sarah Moore said. 'They're bombing London in midnight raids, you know.'

'Just my luck.'

'Lieutenant Regan, what do you make of the German threat? Everyone is talking about it now that we are approaching the war zone. Do you think a submarine will attack us?'

Now Patrick Regan looked uneasy. 'We're not supposed

to talk about it,' he said. 'Captain's orders.'

'But why have there been no lifeboat drills?'

'There was one,' Connie said. 'I saw them practising. They need to do more practise, I think, because they didn't manage it properly.'

Patrick Regan looked sharply at her. Then his face calmed again. 'Tomorrow the lifeboats will all be swung out on their davits. They'll be ready for action at a moment's notice. And remember, we travel at twenty-one knots at present and a submarine can only make about half that, so the chances of one catching us are very slight. On top of that, Captain Turner will probably order the passengers to wear life jackets at all times. That's what we did when I was on the *Mauritania*. It's a common-sense precaution. No more. We really have no need to fear.'

'But if one does catch us,' the American said, 'what then?'

Patrick Regan actually glanced over his shoulder. Connie followed his gaze and saw the rough, stocky form of Captain Turner, uncomfortable in his dark uniform and gold braid. He was listening with a pained expression to an elderly gentleman telling him some obscure and complicated story. Everyone knew he was a sailor's captain, and hated entertaining the passengers. He did not come to the dining room most evenings but dined in his own cabin, leaving the work of dressing up in gold braid and brass buttons to impress the passengers to his junior officers. He looked somehow solid and reliable and trust-worthy, the kind of man who had learned his skills the hard way, the kind of man who would not let you down.

'Everyone thinks of the *Titanic*, of course,' Patrick Regan was saying, 'but remember we have far more lifeboats than we need and they didn't have enough. We could put twice as many people into our lifeboats. And, of course, the *Titanic* proved that it takes hours for a ship this size to sink. And she had a terrific gash all along her side. One or even two torpedoes would not do much damage to a ship as big as old Lucy here. Not with our watertight bulkheads and so forth. Even if she did sink, it would take forever. We would have more than enough time to launch all the boats and get everyone aboard. There is absolutely no need for anxiety.' But Connie detected something in Patrick Regan's eyes that told her that he too was afraid.

'What if they can't launch the boats?' she said. 'Those men I saw got all tangled up.'

He glanced at Captain Turner again. The captain was not in his place. A waiter stood by his empty chair stacking plates on his arm. The elderly gentleman was still there, talking to a younger man. The rest of the table was empty. 'I'm afraid I must go on duty,' Patrick Regan said. 'Though I'm sorry to leave you. It's been a very interesting meal!'

Saturday 6 May 1915

In the Prison Cell

Oisín had been chatting to Old Dunphy, the steward, and had discovered that the old fellow was not as bad as he had originally thought. He knew quite a lot about ships and things, and was able to tell him that Old Lucy, as everyone called her, was originally designed as an auxiliary cruiser. She could be converted 'at the drop of a hat' into a ship of war with twelve six-inch guns. She had the most powerful steam turbine engines ever built, and could do twenty-five knots. On top of all that, she was nearly eight hundred feet long!

'Eight hundred feet!' Oisín gasped. 'Tremendous!'

He thought for a moment. 'How long is that?'

Old Dunphy shook his head. 'Very long.'

'I'll bet it is. I'm going to measure it.'

It was while attempting to pace out the length of the boat-deck – assuming that one of his paces was a bit short of two feet – that Oisín walked straight into Captain Turner who was strolling there, hands clasped behind his back, and nodding to passengers, with a strained look on his face.

'Hey ho! Young man! Steady on there!'

Oisín backed off the great mass of dark serge uniform and stared up at the weather-beaten face of an elderly officer.

'Hey!' he said. 'Watch where you're going!'

'I believe I had the right of way,' Captain Turner said. 'I was on the starboard tack.'

Oisín gave him the kind of look he reserved for Connie when she was being particularly stupid. 'I didn't see any starboard tack.'

'Ah,' Captain Turner said. 'I see you are not familiar with the shipping regulations. You see, the wind is this way,' and he indicated the side of the ship that the wind was coming from. 'That is my starboard side. It is on your port side. You should have kept out of my way. That is the duty of all sailing vessels.'

'But I'm not a vessel at all,' Oisín complained. 'I'm a small boy.'

'A small boy indeed,' Captain Turner agreed. 'But one who does not look where he is going.'

'Sorry,' Oisín said, beginning to feel that he was losing the battle. 'I'll look next time.'

'What exactly were you doing, small boy?'

'I was measuring the ship.'

'A very important job. The kind of thing naval archi-tects do all the time. They make a tidy living out of it too. But we have already had her measured. She is exactly seven hundred and eighty-five feet long from stem to stern.'

'That's what Old Dunphy said. Only he said it was eight hundred feet.'

'Old Dunphy is clearly not as careful about figures as I am. Would you like a lesson in how the shipping regulations work?'

'I suppose I would.' Oisín didn't like the sound of any kind of lesson at all, but having walked straight into the old gentleman, he could hardly refuse. Besides, he was an officer, and Oisín had the clear impression that officers expected to be obeyed.

'I was just going up to the bridge. Follow me.'

'The bridge!' Oisín gasped. 'Up to the bridge?' Was he dreaming? Could it be possible that he, Oisín Moore, had been invited to follow some old officer to the bridge of the *Lusitania*?

But Captain Turner was already stalking off. He led Oisín by a series of ladders and stairways right up to the top of the ship, where, stepping through a glass door, Oisín found himself in the most beautiful room he had ever seen. It was twice as long as their dining room at Ballyshane House, with bright windows all along the front and sides, and an array of gleaming brass instruments and levers, compasses and bells. The sound of the engines did not reach this far at all, and the room was filled with a kind of sunlit quiet, disturbed occasionally by some slight clicking from another room. Previously he had thought the engine room was heaven; now he revised his opinion. This was heaven indeed.

Captain Turner introduced him to several officers and sailors who seemed to have nothing better to do than stand about looking out through the windows. Following their gaze, Oisín saw the entire forward part of the ship stretched out like an enormous broad arrow in front of him, the wake streaming out from the bows on either side, a great foaming tide that stretched away out of his vision and fell behind the ship. 'This is a small boy who has been measuring our ship. I've decided to show him what the *Lusitania* looks like from the captain's point of view.' The other officers and sailors laughed and nodded to him. One officer said, 'Welcome to the bridge, young chap.'

'Where is the old man, Old Turner?' Oisín asked. 'Our steward, Old Dunphy, says he spends all his time in bed.'

This remark was greeted by a strained silence. One of the officers coughed into his hand and pretended to have seen something on the starboard bow. A sailor turned away.

Captain Turner placed himself directly in front of Oisín, hands in his jacket pocket, feet planted wide apart. 'Young man, before we go any further, perhaps we should introduce ourselves. Then you can explain to me exactly who this "Old Dunphy" of yours is, and we can put him right on his numbers and various other things.'

Oisín stuck out his hand and shook Captain Turner's hand warmly. 'Oisín Moore,' he said. 'Oisín after a poem by a Dublin fellow. I keep forgetting his name.'

'William Turner,' Captain Turner said. 'Captain of the *Lusitania*.'

Oisín went pale. 'I say, I'm really sorry,' he said. 'Crumbs! I'm in for it now!'

'Never mind, young man,' Captain Turner said. 'I can see you need a lot of educating. Now give me the number of your cabin, and I'll send a chap down to let your parents know where we are. That way no one will be worrying. I'll have you properly educated by dinner time.' Turning to one of the other officers he said, 'I think we'll drop this Old Dunphy chap over the side at about eight bells, eh?' Everyone chuckled.

'Don't go telling everyone on the ship I brought you up here, young fellow,' Captain Turner told him. 'Otherwise we'll have every Tom, Dick and Harry looking for an invitation. I only brought you because I thought you had a naval architect sort of look about you, all this measuring of the ship and so on.'

Three hours later Oisín was telling Tom Boland and Connie about his experience. 'He showed me the whole place. Where the helm is.' He said 'helm' very carefully, having heard the word only that afternoon. 'And where the navigator fellow is and all. He let me steer.'

'Oh, you're a terrible liar,' Connie said. 'He never let you steer.'

'He did. He did. He let me steer for five minutes, only we were just going straight ahead, so I couldn't turn her or anything. But I was still steering. That's what the other fellow was doing too. The other helm.'

Then he remembered the greatest treat of all. 'He gave me tea and buns in the captain's day cabin.'

Connie's eyes opened wide in amazement. 'Tea and buns?'

'That's what he always has for tea,' Oisín said. 'Sticky buns.'

Connie laughed outright. 'He does not! A captain of a ship would never eat sticky buns!'

'He does! He does!' Oisín cried. 'Tea and buns, he has!'

'Well, that's it so,' Connie said. 'That proves it. You never were up there at all.'

Tom Boland said, 'You're only codding us.'

Oisín was almost in tears. 'You're just jealous.'

He stalked away to find the steward, the only adult who was likely to listen to his story. He knew that his mother was playing cards in some ladies' room or other.

Old Dunphy believed him straight away. 'The old man is not so bad,' he said. 'He has a family of his own.'

'He told me that. He had a picture in his day cabin.'

Oisín was sitting on the edge of his bed while Old Dunphy swept the floor.

'Did he tell you about the spies?'

Oisín was suddenly all ears. 'What spies? He never said anything about spies.'

'Oh, maybe I better say nothing, so,' Old Dunphy said. 'I better be going.'

'Oh, please, Mr Dunphy!' Old Dunphy actually had his hand on the door handle, and Oisín felt an urgent need to stop him leaving. He knew from experience that if the steward walked out he might never hear any more of this intriguing news. It had already happened before, when the old man had walked right out in the middle of telling Oisín how he had been caught by a giant squid and almost pulled over the side. Just when he came to the bit about cutting away the squid's tentacles. Try as he might, Oisín had never been able to get the rest of the story out of him. 'Please! What spies? Oh *please*, Mr Dunphy. I won't tell anyone, I promise.' The steward seemed to let the handle go reluctantly. He turned back and came over to where Oisín was sitting. He bent down so that his mouth was level with Oisín's ear, and whispered, 'Three of 'em. Hiding in a storeroom.'

Oisín's eyes popped wide open. 'Stowaways?'

'So you might say.'

'But you said spies.'

'That's what we thinks.'

'German?'

Old Dunphy shook his head. 'Can't get nothing out of them. They didn't say a word since we caught them.'

'To hide their accent?'

'That's what we thinks.'

'Did they have guns? Or a bomb?'

Again Old Dunphy shook his head. 'Crew searched the whole ship, stem to stern, top to bottom. Not a thing.'

'So they were unarmed.'

'Nothing found, anyway.'

'Oh.'

'We thinks it might be something to do with the attack.'

Oisín gasped. 'What attack?'

'The notice. The German notice.'

'You mean the notice was a trick. They never meant to attack by submarine.'

'Right. Be useless, wouldn't it? Them old tubs couldn't catch old Lucy. She's too fast. They'd have to get her some other way. So they sent spies. Only we caught them first.'

'But if they didn't have a bomb...'

'Right you are. But what if they was to sabotage the machinery. Wreck the engines? Or open a seacock and flood the ship?'

'Oh.'

'Anyway,' Old Dunphy said, straightening up, 'we

caught the so-and-sos, didn't we? Begod we did. And the old man says, 'Clap 'em in irons!' he does. And that's where they are. Down in the hold, chained up and mighty sad looking.'

'Have you seen them?'

'I been down to look at them. A right trio.'

Oisín looked pleadingly at Old Dunphy. 'Could I see them?' But the steward shook his head. 'Can't do it, mate. Captain's orders.'

'Aw!' Oisín wailed. 'It's so unfair!'

'Never you mind, young man,' Old Dunphy said. 'You still saw the bridge, didn't you?' And he was gone, closing the door behind him. Oisín could hear him saying 'Good evening' to someone in the passageway outside.

It was exciting that Old Lucy had spies on her. Oisín thought that he was never again likely to be on such an exciting ship. And he believed that they were German spies. But then he thought that spies would have weapons and would be ready to fight their way out at all costs. And what kind of spies would be planning to sink a ship like this, an auxiliary cruiser, with their bare hands? Surely the Imperial German Navy had enough bombs to spare to give one to their spies?

No, the more he thought about it, the more convinced he became that these men were not spies at all. What then?

Suddenly he remembered Sir Hugh Lane and his fabulously valuable paintings. Hadn't he said that they were locked away in a lead box in the hold? And wasn't that exactly where Captain Turner had put the spies? What if that was part of their plan? What if they escaped from their chains and stole the paintings? Sir Hugh would be most upset.

He, Oisín Moore, had pledged himself to defend that lead box. It was now his duty to investigate the spy business and pass on any information he had to Sir Hugh and the captain. This was what Father would have said, he knew. Father was very strong on duty. That was why he had volunteered to fight for Ireland and Mr Redmond. It was his duty, he said. Oisín pulled on his shoes, which he had taken off because the new leather in them was chafing his ankle, and opened the door carefully. There was no sign of Old Dunphy. He slipped along the corridor to where a door on the left said, 'No Passengers Beyond this Point. By Order of the Captain.' He opened the door and slipped inside.

He found himself in the middle of a crude steel staircase full of the smell of oil and stale clothes. By a weak light he could see that the walls were pimpled everywhere with the heads of rivets. The stairs fell away almost vertically below him, and in the slight heave of the ship he thought he would pitch forward and down into the black hole. He held onto the steel sides and stepped down, feeling below him for the next step. There seemed to be a very long gap, and at first he wondered if there was a step at all. At last, his hesitant foot found some-thing solid. He took another step. He supposed that these ladders were not meant for boys, but grown men who did not mind big gaps. He stepped down again, becoming more confident with each step. Down and down he went, passing other doors that led into the second-class and third-class decks. At last he knew by the huge grumbling of the engine that he had sunk down below the passenger level. He was nervous and thought that the sound of his own heart was louder than the big steam turbines. On his right was a door with a brass wheel that operated a series of iron bars. He turned the wheel and saw the bars move, unlocking a dark opening. Now he was in an even more gloomy grey-painted corridor. The engine noise was almost a scream here.

He closed the door behind him and began to make his way forward, away from the noise. Once or twice he passed other corridors that ran at right angles, and expected to see people, sailors going about their business, to be caught even, someone shouting to him to go back, wanting to know what he was doing down here. They were deserted except for the constant vibration and a curious feeling of dust hovering in the air. Why was there no one else down there? Where were all the men who worked the ship? It came into Oisín's head that something had happened, that the ship had struck an iceberg and was sinking and that all the passengers and crew had been taken off, that he was alone on this huge monster and she was going to the bottom. The thought frightened him so much that he put his hand on his heart to stop it from jumping right out of his breast.

He told himself that it was May and there were no icebergs in the water in summer. Then it occurred to him that perhaps a submarine had caught them. Perhaps the crew were launching the lifeboats at this very minute and the submarine was about to fire. He stopped and listened for a moment in case he might hear the blast. But the ship's noises were unchanged. Somewhere far away, he thought, the Germans are gathering, but not here. He was safe for the moment.

'If they do torpedo us while I'm down here, I shall never jolly well find my way out! That's me done for, anyway!' he thought.

'Don't be silly,' he told himself then. He thought he sounded just like Father. 'Don't be silly, Oisín,' Father used to say. 'It's only a shadow.' He didn't remember his father too well sometimes. Two years is a long time in the life of a nine-year-old, and when Father did come home on leave from the war it was for such a short time. Oisín wished he could be at home all the time, even though he was fiercely proud of the fact that his father was a flier, flying high above the war and battling it out like a knight on his charger with the German fliers, who were, according to Father, brave chaps also.

He had stopped in his tracks when the thought about the iceberg occurred to him. Now, coming back to his senses, he found himself outside a door that said 'Cells. No Admittance.'

'Golly,' he said. 'I'm here.'

He opened the door carefully and peeped in. He expected a sailor to be on guard, perhaps with a revolver, but there was no one on duty. He pushed the heavy steel door open, stepped inside and closed it firmly but silently behind him. The room he was in was freezing, probably, he realised, because it was well below the waterline. The heat of the engines did not reach this far forward and down. The thought of the ocean rushing by outside the steel walls, outside but also above his head, made him shiver. He had noticed as he walked along the corridor that the walls were damp with condensation, like the inside of a cave.

There were four cells. Each cell door had a small grille high up – too high for Oisín to see in – at about the place where an adult could look. He glanced around and found a stool which he dragged towards the first door.

Standing on the stool he was barely able to look above the bottom of the grille. It took a moment for his eyes to adjust to the gloom of the interior. The cell was empty except for four bare beds and some kind of bucket.

He dragged the stool to the second door. That cell too was empty. He was beginning to wonder if Old Dunphy had been pulling his leg.

But when his eyes adjusted to the dim light of the third cell he was able to make out the shapes of three men lying on the bunks, covered in brown blankets. Suddenly his knees began to shake and he had to step down. He sat on the stool and wondered what he should do. In the end he decided he should talk. At least he should ask them who they were. They might reveal something to him, knowing that he was a child, in the way that adults sometimes said things in the belief that children could not understand.

'Hello,' he called, stepping up on the stool again. 'I say! You fellows!'

When he looked through the grille he was startled to see a man's face close up to it, no more than inches away. He felt the man's breath before he fell backwards off the stool and landed sprawled against the far side.

'Wot you want, eh?' the man said, hostile, almost shouting. 'Eh? Wot?'

'Sorry,' Oisín said, feeling immediately foolish because it was really the man who should be apologising for knocking him down. 'Excuse me.' He got up.

The man obviously thought Oisín was leaving. 'Oi!' he shouted. 'Wot you want then?'

Oisín looked carefully around him to make sure the man could not escape, and said, 'Are you a spy?'

The man laughed. 'Shove off!'

The face disappeared from the grille.

'Are you art thieves?' Oisín blurted it out, desperate to keep the man talking. He said it without thinking.

The reaction from inside the cell was startling. Three voices erupted in shouting.

'That's the last bloody straw, that is!'

'God's blood! Wot next?'

''Oo's callin' us thieves?'

The face reappeared at the grille. 'If I 'ad you in 'ere I'd twist yer bloody neck off, lad.'

'Sorry,' Oisín said again. 'I was just wondering. If you're not spies or thieves, what are you doing down here? I mean, in the prison?'

There was a short, muttered conversation from inside the door, then another face appeared at the grille. ''Ere, any chance of you getting us a bit o' grub, then? A nice bit o' meat? Give you two bob for it, for a whopping great piece o' meat. How 'bout it, then? We don't get nothing down 'ere only bread an' stuff. Man cannot live on bread alone, eh?'

Oisín had an idea.

'All right,' he said. 'I'll get you some meat after lunch tomorrow, but only if you tell me the truth about why you're on this ship.'

There was another short, muttered conversation. The first man emerged now, his face pressed against the bars of the grille.

'Righto, chum. We'll tell you when you bring the meat.'

'No,' Oisín said. They were fools to think a nine-year-old boy with a big sister would be fooled by that old trick. How often had Connie promised something, provided he did this or that, and then when he had done it, run away laughing? Too often. 'No,' he told the men. 'You're in there and I'm out here. Tell me now or I won't bother about the meat.'

The man said, 'You're a bleedin' 'ard bargain, chum, no doubt about it. I s'pose it can't do any 'arm anyway. Wot you fink, boys?'

They all seemed to agree.

'We're stowaways, ain't we? Stowed away for a trip back to Blighty. Now it looks like we're going to see Dear Old England from the windows of Wandsworth Prison.'

'Is that all?'

'That's it.'

'But why did they put you in here?'

The man shook his head and his face appeared and disappeared from the grille. 'That bleedin' captain cove, what's-'is-name . . . ?

'Turner? Captain Turner?'

'No . . . the other one, the staff captain cove, Anderson or something. He wouldn't listen to us, would 'e. You'll upset the passengers, says he. So 'e made out we was German spies. 'E made out we never said a word, didn't 'e? Well the truth is, he couldn't bleedin' shut us up, could 'e?'

'Old Dunphy says you're spies for the Germans.'

"'Oo's Old Dunphy when 'e's at 'ome then?'

'He's a steward.'

'I'll break 'is bleedin' face for 'im if I catch 'im. Tell 'im that.'

Now a second face appeared at the grill.

'We were on our way to join up, that's what. We been in America, see. We were going in for the Army. Now we ain't ever going to get there.'

'I'd better go,' Oisín said. 'I'll be missed.'

'Oi! Don't forget the bleedin' meat!'

One of the men inside the cell shouted, 'We ain't done nothin'! Nothin'!'

'That's right!' the face at the door said. 'We're innocent men!'

SUNDAY 7 MAY 1915

THE MORNING OF ANOTHER GLORIOUS DAY

It would be another beautiful day once the fog burned off. Walter Schwieger was enjoying the fresh air in the conning tower. He had four men posted there, conscious that now they were in the sea lanes off the south coast of Ireland. He had the submarine running on slow ahead, because in the fog they could see nothing. She was making no more than seven knots through the water and the tide was against them, making it perhaps six, or even five and a half knots, really. He was not worried. The last thing he wanted was to go blundering at high speed into some invisible rock because the navigation was a few kilometres wrong. Or worse, if *U-20* ran straight into a ship at high speed! He chewed on a piece of black bread and drank the bitter coffee the cook had brewed for him, while pondering his orders. So far the voyage had not been a great success. One shipload of horses and one ancient wooden schooner! Not targets he could boast about at home. In between there had been the usual gut-wrenching cat-and-mouse game with destroyers and submarine chasers, together with some pure terror from patches of fog and other imaginary enemies. He had not yet reached his cruising ground, and already he was half-worn-out, and so was the crew.

Their cruising ground was the approach to Liverpool, where the High Command believed they would find rich pickings. Should he set course directly for Liverpool, or follow the steamer track along the south coast of Ireland? Otto Lanz had shown him the plot an hour ago and, according to that excellent navigator, they were now west of a place called the Old Head of Kinsale. Walter Schwieger wondered idly why it should be called the 'old' head. Was there a 'new' head nearby, one that had perhaps risen from the sea unexpectedly in recent years? Or had Kinsale itself been moved, and so come nearer to some other headland?

'The fog is beginning to lift, *Herr Oberleutnant*,' one of the lookouts said, and, gazing hard at the fog on that side, it was possible to see a distant patch of sunlight on a calm sea. Yes, breaks were appearing. Somewhere, high above the cold, clammy air, the sun burned brightly, warming the earth, air and water, but not yet extending its kindness to submarine *U-20*. Ah well, Walter Schwieger thought, that is the submariner's life – cold and damp while others bask in the sunshine.

Otto Lanz came up, surveyed the blank, grey wall and said, '*Herr Oberleutnant*, it was reported that the fog is lifting. I had hoped to sight land and get a position fix.' Walter Schwieger noticed that Otto held his sextant in his hand, intending to use some landmark like this Old Head to fix his position. The technique, known as 'horizontal sextant angles', was Otto's favourite piece of navigation. Nothing gave him more pleasure than marking the tiny spot on a chart and saying, 'Yes, this is where we are *exactly.*' Walter Schwieger could well imagine him doing the same with some piece of ancient Greek translation and saying, 'Yes, this is what it means *exactly.*' It would drive his students mad when he got back to Heidelberg and took up his post as lecturer – a post that would surely come his way after the war.

Walter Schwieger gestured at the blankness that surrounded them and then at the brighter patch to starboard. 'As you see, Otto, the fog has not lifted. I will send for you when it does, yes?'

Otto lingered for a moment, looking as though there was something he wanted to say, but in the end he said nothing and disappeared down the hatch into the dark, fuggy interior again.

When the fog did clear it cleared in patches, so that one minute *U-20* was steaming through total invisibility, so thick that the bow of the submarine could scarcely be seen from the conning tower, and the next the bow was sliding out into brilliant sunshine, and for perhaps half a kilometre there was blue sky, warmth and a glittering sea. On one such occasion they identified the Old Head of Kinsale, and Otto Lanz was sent for. He brought his sextant, a notebook and a folded chart and spent a happy five minutes reading angles to one of the lookouts, who noted them down. Then he vanished below, to re-emerge ten minutes later, triumphantly waving his notebook.

'*Herr Oberleutnant*, I know *exactly* where we are now. This has been good. A good position. That,' he said, pointing east-north-east into the fog that had closed in once again, 'is the Old Head of Kinsale. As we expected, yes? It is twenty-one kilometres away.' He was like a child with a new toy, full of boyish excitement. 'So. We know where we are.'

'Good, Otto. Very good. In this fog, I thought we might not get a fix.'

Otto beamed around him for a minute and then went below again.

Captain Turner was uneasy, Oisín could see that. The captain was pacing up and down on the bridge, glaring out at the blank white wall that was the window. The fog was so thick that Oisín had almost got lost on his way up. He had been invited by Captain Turner to view the fog clearing from the bridge of Old Lucy. It was a wonderful sight, he had been told, to watch the bow of the ship, which at present could not be seen, slowly emerge from its shroud of grey, and the surrounding sea turn from grey to bright blue. The fog had been confidently expected to lift before ten o'clock. But it had not lifted. And Captain Turner seemed to have forgotten the presence of the small boy.

Oisín watched everything with awe. He saw Lieutenant Patrick Regan come and say that the glass was steady and the water temperature hadn't changed. The two men moved to one side of the bridge – the side near Oisín, as it happened – and he heard Patrick Regan say something about a signal from the Admiralty at Queenstown. 'Damn them!' Captain Turner had said. 'Look at that, man. No submarine could find us in this. We don't know where we are ourselves.'

'Oh Captain, I'm sure Mr Hanson is correct in his navigation. He always is.'

'Yes, yes. But what if he isn't. Ireland is out there, sir. And that's a lot of rock.'

One of the sailors looked at Oisín and winked. 'The old man is always nervous in fog,' he whispered. 'Pay no heed to 'im.'

But Patrick Regan was saying that they should zigzag. 'Orders from the Admiralty, sir,' he said. 'We should zigzag and stay offshore.'

'Blast them!' Captain Turner roared. 'Bloody Admiral Coke. What does old Coke know about it? Even his fastest ship couldn't keep up with the *Lusitania*. We're faster than any of them. Anyway,' in a lower voice, 'if we zigzag now, in the fog, who knows where we will end up. No. Besides, I hope to raise the land any moment. We will get a clear fix on something ashore, and then we will know how accurate Mr Hanson's navigation is.'

'Eighteen knots, sir,' a man standing by some instruments said. 'Chief reports all well.'

'Very good,' Captain Turner said. 'We will maintain eighteen knots. We can't afford to go blundering around at high speed in these shipping lanes. Slow, that's the word. Take her slow.' Then, as an afterthought, 'Bring up your sextant, Mr Regan. We'll sight the Old Head of Kinsale shortly, as soon as this pea-souper clears away. The practise will do you good.'

'Now, this will be our last day on the boat,' Sarah Moore said. 'We will be in Liverpool tomorrow. So I've decided that we will all eat lunch together. How about that?'

Connie nodded her head unenthusiastically. Sarah studied her face for a moment, then smiled. 'Oh all right, you can bring your young friend with you. Yes, we'll have him to lunch as well.'

'Oh, can we?' Connie cried, her facing lighting up

suddenly. 'Oh Mother, thank you.'

'Run along, child,' Sarah Moore said, thinking to herself as she said it that Connie was no longer so much a child, but a girl growing into womanhood. She was only thirteen, but in many ways she was as mature and sensible as any adult. And besides, young Tom Boland was a nice boy, and his parents, to whom she had recently been introduced, were nice people also. She could not think of a better friend for her Connie than young Tom Boland.

Connie went out to stare at the unbroken wall of fog. She hoped that if she stared hard enough, she would see some indication that the beloved shore was out there, some hint of green hillsides, or the brown of frost-burnt heather that would mean home. But the fog was un-remitting. Many passengers had been up since dawn, hoping to catch their first glimpse of home. It was an hour since the ship had made a turn to the right, which she knew meant that they were running along the south coast. She tried to remember the names of places along that coast, but could name only two: Cork and Kinsale. Perhaps they were passing Cork even now.

'Hey, Connie!' It was Oisín, returned, rather put out, from the bridge. 'I was up on the bridge.'

'I know. Mother told me.'

'It wasn't much fun.'

Connie sniffed and put on her I-don't-care face. 'I expect it wasn't.'

'No, but we couldn't see anything.'

'Neither can anybody else.'

'Yes, but the captain is fierce about it. He's like a hen with an egg.'

Connie said, 'That's one of May's sayings. I remember her saying that.' The mention of May seemed to unite them. They imagined her, at this moment, sitting at home in the warm kitchen of Ballyshane, knitting or darning, or cooking one of her enormous lunches.

More kindly, Connie said, 'Was the captain angry, so?'

'He was!' Oisín said eagerly. 'Old Patrick Regan said that Admiral Someone-or-other was after saying that the ship should be zigzagging and Old Turner said damn them. He said he couldn't zigzag because he didn't know where we are. We're supposed to keep far off the shore in case of submarines, well out to sea, but the old man says we have to get in close to get a position.' The word 'position' was his newest treasure. He had heard the officers use it several times that morning. It was something they were very concerned about. He knew that from their worried faces and the way they sort of lowered their voices when they mentioned it. He hoped Connie would ask him what it meant.

'What's zigzagging?'

Oisín was first disappointed that 'position' hadn't come up, then shocked when he realised he didn't actually know what zigzagging was. 'Oh,' he said casually, 'keeping a sharp lookout for submarines and ramming them if we see them. That's zigzagging. That's what I'm doing until lunchtime. I'm on lookout duty for zigzagging.'

'Oh.'

'For submarines.'

'If this fog doesn't clear up you won't be able to see much.'

'Look!' Oisín shouted. 'There's a clear patch. Over

there.' He pointed and Connie saw a patch of sea on which it appeared to her the sun had scattered the most brilliant diamonds she had ever seen.

'Alarm! Alarm!' The shout reverberated through the hull. Walter Schwieger was in the tower in a matter of seconds. It was Rueff again, pointing to the west. He handed his Zeiss glasses to Walter Schwieger and waited.

Walter Schwieger studied the western horizon through the beautiful clarity of the lens. He saw clumps of fog like isolated sheep on a blue field. Apart from that and the land to the north, the sea appeared empty.

'What?' he said.

'Smoke, *Herr Oberleutnant*. I think I saw smoke. A lot of smoke, like from two or three funnels.'

Walter Schwieger thought Rueff had seen fog but he knew that everyone's nerves were on edge, and so he said, 'Good, Rueff. That will be a big one, yes? Keep looking. Call me if you see anything else.'

He went below and told the men to relax again. Nothing yet.

Otto Lanz was looking at him with that expectant look, a pencil in his hand.

'Nothing, Otto. Just the fog, I think. Gunther Rueff thought he saw a three-funnel ship, or at least the smoke from one. But there is nothing there.'

'A three-funnel ship?' Otto Lanz repeated. 'Something big. A passenger liner, perhaps.' There was an unspoken question in his eyes. They both knew the High Command had ordered unrestricted warfare. Yet no one had delib-erately attacked a big passenger ship. It seemed somehow beyond the requirements of war. 'Yes, *Herr Oberleutnant*, that could be a passenger liner,' he repeated, still gazing steadily at Walter Schwieger.

'Let us hope it is,' Walter Schwieger said with studied brutality. 'A big fat liner with a thousand passengers. It would be nice to sink something worthwhile like that, yes?'

A wave of revulsion passed over Otto Lanz's face, and Walter Schwieger knew that he had finally forfeited the friendship of that intelligent man. No matter, he thought, I am the captain and he is the pilot. I am a fighting man and always have been. He is a scholar. I will do what I have to do.

But now he was surprised that the hardening of his heart had proceeded so well without him knowing it. He found himself wishing for the appearance of this unknown, invisible three-funnel ship, laden with Britishers, so that he could send it to the bottom. He was more than a little shocked at himself. Had he become a glory hunter after all this time? Did he hope to achieve fame by one enormous blow? Or had be become a true monster, ready to kill and maim for some kind of pleasure? Walter Schwieger realised that he did not know himself. He felt lost. Where was the man he had been? Where was the officer who had cared for his men, who hated to sink a ship without allowing the crew time to escape? What had become of that other Walter Schwieger? He shook his head in amazement.

'I am tired, Otto. It has been a long voyage. I will not be sorry when we can turn for home again.'

Otto Lanz looked at his captain, and saw the lines on his face that were the marks of a year and a half of cruising below the surface, attacking faster ships and watching men drown through the cold, gleaming lens of the periscope. He did not look like a hero or a warrior, he looked like a man who had been working too hard. A businessman who had stayed too late at the office, too often. Nothing like Hector or Achilles.

Otto Lanz turned away in disgust. For the first time ever he saw his captain as human, and that meant that he too, and all the crew, were human. That this trade they were involved in was no more than the grubby killing of men that they had never seen. There was nothing heroic about it. The thought left a bad taste in his mouth. A sour taste, like wine that had turned acid in the bottle.

'The fog is clearing, dear,' Linda Davis said, coming up to Sarah, where she stood near the grand entrance. 'Soon we'll be able to see your Emerald Isle.'

'Yes,' Sarah said. 'I think I've seen it already. Over there.'

'It'll be on the other side, ma'am,' a passing sailor said. 'You're on the port side now. The land'll be over on the starboard side. Other side of the ship altogether.'

'My goodness,' Sarah Moore said. 'That fog sure does have me confused.'

She and Linda Davis strolled together to the other side of the ship, and were just in time to see her burst through the gloom and out into the open. Suddenly, they were looking across a bright sea towards the distant coast of Ireland, little more than a blue line at present, but judging by the direction the ship was taking it would soon be clear enough. The bow seemed to be pointed straight at a long, high headland with a lighthouse at its end.

'What a glorious day!' she said. 'God, I love that little country.'

'I can see that,' Linda Davis said. 'It looks pretty enough.'

Sarah Moore turned to her friend. 'You must come over and stay with us at Ballyshane, Linda. You should see my garden in summer – rhododendrons, azaleas, fuchsia. There's no place in the world like it.'

Linda laughed. 'You sound so Irish,' she said.

'I am Irish,' Sarah Moore said. 'Now.'

'God damn, what is it now?' Walter Schwieger shouted as he emerged from the hatch. Up here the sunshine was warm. He made a note that when he calmed down he would allow the men to come out onto the deck in groups of four to stretch their backs and enjoy the day. 'What is it now?'

Gunther Rueff was staring through his binoculars, but even with the naked eye Walter Schwieger could see that this time it *was* a ship, a big one too. 'Well?' he barked.

'*Herr Oberleutnant*, I wish to report a four-funnel steamer.'

'Are you mad?' Walter Schwieger grabbed the binoculars and focused them. Rueff was right. She was a four-funnel steamer. 'Tell Herr Lanz to come up immediately,' he told Rueff calmly.

Otto Lanz came up and stared for a moment through the Zeiss. 'Well, Otto?' Walter Schwieger asked. 'You will consult your book, yes?'

Otto Lanz shook his head. 'I do not need to, *Herr Oberleutnant*. Even so far away her lines are unmistakable. See, she has the narrow lines and hull of a warship. A cruiser, I think. Yet she is clearly a passenger steamer.'

'What are you saying?'

'She can only be one of two ships, *Herr Oberleutnant*. She is either the *Mauritania* or the *Lusitania*. Cunard Line. It is impossible that she should be anything else.'

Otto Lanz put down the binoculars and stared at the sea. Walter Schwieger knew he was thinking about him, but the pilot looked only straight ahead. There was a kind of hurt anger in his face. The captain knew that Otto Lanz did not approve of the order to sink such ships.

'Well, it seems we will not have to worry about her. She is steaming away from us. I estimate her speed at twenty knots. She will cross our bows far out of range. Relax, Otto. Your soul will not be tested yet.' He slapped the pilot on the back and laughed aloud, but the pilot did not laugh.

And even as they watched, the four-funnel ship altered course towards them.

The two men stared in shock for a moment.

'My God! Look at that! She turns towards us!' Walter Schwieger could not keep the delight from his voice. Otto Lanz murmured something about their course and disappeared down the hatch. Walter Schwieger did not have the time to wonder about his reactions. He turned to the lookouts and said, 'Hurry! Down! She will pass within range of us. Go!'

He shouted the order to submerge and took one last look through the binoculars to make sure that he had not been dreaming. No, she had turned. She was steaming towards them as merrily as if it were peacetime. Then he climbed down the ladder and closed the hatch over his head.

U-20 dived out of the sunlight and into the green sea.

SUNDAY 7 MAY 1915

LUNCHEON

A frosty indifference had prevailed between Mrs Sarah Moore and the man the children called Batface since the night of the quarrelsome dinner party. Now they met as Mrs Moore was leaving the lounge and he was entering it. Meeting exactly at the door, they were required to stop, he to let her pass, but, confused by the confrontation, he simply stood in front of her.

'Excuse me, sir,' Sarah Moore said coldly. 'I am on my way to luncheon in the dining room.'

'I beg your pardon, ma'am,' Batface said, removing a straw boater hat, raising it about six inches above his head and stepping aside. Then, as Sarah brushed past him, he said, 'I owe you an apology, ma'am.'

The words stopped Sarah in her tracks. She turned to look at the man and saw that his face was working like someone who was about to burst into tears. Shocked, she said, 'Thank you, sir. I accept your apology.'

'You see,' he said, 'I was ... overwrought. Yes, over-wrought.' He repeated the word, as though it had only just occurred to him that this was an exact description of his state of mind at the time. 'I was very overwrought indeed.'

'I understand,' Sarah Moore said. She did not understand, but she wanted to get away from the embarrassing situation as quickly as possible. People were beginning to come out of the lounge now, making for the dining room for the first sitting, and they were looking with curiosity at the little scene between the Englishman and the Irish-American woman.

'No, no,' he cried. 'Please. Allow me to explain.' He gestured towards the nearest chairs in the lounge. 'I won't detain you for long.'

With an almost silent sigh, Sarah sat down. The lounge was a sumptuous room, with a rich green carpet that was as restful to the eye as the green of a lawn. The walls were panelled in mahogany and the chairs were deep and comfortable. Sunlight flooded in through the windows, and fell like a blessing on the people relaxing there.

'You see, I have two sons. *Had* two sons, actually. They volunteered. Yes, they volunteered at the outbreak of war. One of them was killed at Ypres. Donald. Poor Donald. He was his mother's favourite. Quite the pet. It was a shell ... From our own side. The artillery got it wrong, the ranging. Ranging is so important for artillery. If they don't calculate exactly where the shell will fall, and it lands short, you know ... Or if they don't know exactly where our boys are. Of course, after an explosion like that ... Naturally, there was nothing to bring home. He was just gone. His commanding officer was very polite about it. But I did see some action myself, in the Crimea. It seems a long time ago now. I *understood*. He didn't need to tell me. I knew what that shell would do. We put his name on the family grave. Just his name. He's not in it, of course, but it's a comfort. Just to look at the name sometimes. His mother, of course, was devastated. Devastated.'

There were tears in the man's eyes.

'Sometimes I get upset, and I say things. I know I do. I go too far. Please allow me to apologise.'

'My husband is in France,' Sarah Moore said, and she, too, meant it as a kind of apology. Immediately, the man's blush of shame deepened and invaded his entire face.

'My God! How callous of me. Of course. I should have known. I beg your pardon.'

'No,' Sarah said. 'We were both cruel, sir. I mention my husband only to explain my own behaviour. I, too, owe you an apology. Please tell me, how is your other son?'

'Campbell? Campbell is alive and well. Was alive and well three weeks ago.' The man's face paled again. 'One never knows from day to day.'

They rose and shook hands. 'I wish you well, sir. I hope your son is returned hale and hearty to you when the war is over.'

'Pray God that is soon. And I trust your husband will return safely.'

'Goodbye.'

'Goodbye.'

Connie met Sarah at the door. 'Mother! Oisín and I have been waiting for you. Tom isn't allowed to come to lunch, and the head waiter refused to seat us until you came!'

'Silly man,' Sarah Moore said, glaring at the head waiter. 'Doesn't he know we're a family, for God's sake!'

She took Connie's hand and held it tight. 'Say a prayer

for Daddy tonight, honey, will you?'

Connie scolded her mother. 'You know I do every night, Mother. I never forget that.'

'I guess I worry sometimes,' Sarah said.

'You mustn't,' Connie told her, feeling very grown up, comforting her mother. 'Father is too clever to be hurt.'

Oisín came along the deck towards them. 'I saw a submarine!' he told them, his face contorted into a deep frown. 'Over there, out to sea. I saw one and I told one of the officers and he said not to be annoying him and to run along and play! I was on lookout and I saw it and he didn't!' Anger was adding volume to his voice. He was wailing now. 'It was a black submarine!'

'Stop that at once!' Sarah said. 'People will hear!'

'But I did!' Tears spilled over and ran down his cheeks. 'And they didn't take any notice, and we're supposed to be zigzagging and they never said "Put on the life jackets"!'

'Nonsense!' Sarah Moore hissed. 'Look up there.' She pointed at the wing of the bridge, where they could see a sailor with a pair of binoculars scanning the sea on all sides. 'Don't you think if there was a submarine there, he would have seen it first?'

This obvious truth silenced Oisín. And of course it was impossible to believe that there could be any danger out there. The sea glittered in the midday sun, each tiny wavelet sparkling like a piece of silver or shining steel. There was almost no swell, and the coast looked serene and warm. Over there, people were sitting down to their Sunday dinners. Their houses were full of the warm smell of cooking, doors and windows thrown wide open to welcome the glorious season in. People would be picnicking by the seaside and watching the great four-funnelled liner glide by on a perfect ocean.

'I did see something,' Oisín said, wiping a big, round tear from his eye. 'I suppose it might have been a whale.'

Later, over lunch, it had become 'the most enormous whale' that rolled and dived and surfaced again, and blew a great fountain into the air. Linda Davis, who had stopped to chat, was very impressed. She seemed knowledgeable too, and enquired whether he thought it was a sperm whale or a blue whale.

'Oh, I'd say it was a black whale,' Oisín said. 'It certainly wasn't blue.'

'Did you know that I lived in Seattle, Washington for a while? We used to see whales there quite a lot. I once saw a humpback whale come right out of the water. He was bigger than our boat.'

'What kind of a boat was it?' Oisín wanted to know.

'It was a sailing boat belonging to a friend of mine. We were on a sailing trip. I was quite frightened.'

'I bet it was a humpback that I saw too,' he said. 'Only it didn't jump or anything. It just sort of dived. But it had a sort of hump on its back.'

Sarah and Linda exchanged worried looks.

'Did you point it out to anyone, dear?'

'I did,' Oisín told them. 'I said it to a sailor, one of the lookouts. He said to run away and play. But Captain Turner told me to keep a lookout too, you know.'

Sarah and Linda looked relieved. 'So you told someone? That's all right then.'

Linda left them to sit at another table and they settled down to the food. Oisín had not forgotten his promise to the prisoners in the hold to bring them meat. He ordered a prodigious amount of the cold Cumberland ham and wrapped it in his napkin under the table when Sarah was distracted by another of her friends. Connie saw it but didn't say a thing. Sometimes Connie was a good sport!

'Look, Mother,' Connie said. 'There's that horrible old bat-faced man you had the row with the other night. Over there.'

Sarah turned and nodded her head stiffly to Batface, who bowed stiffly back.

'You mustn't say such things about the poor man,' Sarah said. 'He has his own troubles.'

Connie gave her mother a curious glance. 'But he was so horrible. Going on about cowards and traitors. It was such bad manners.'

'He lost his son in France, you know. And his second son is still out there. He was overwrought that night. He has apologised.'

Silence descended on the table.

Captain Turner was in a cheerful mood. They had got a clear position from the Old Head of Kinsale, and Hanson's navigation had proved exact.

Now he intended to follow the inshore course along the south coast, navigating from headland to headland and then round the corner of Wexford and up the Irish Sea to Liverpool. Passengers liked to travel along near the shore after the boredom of a long ocean trip, when there was nothing to see for days except sea and more sea. They would spend their time trying to identify parts of the thin line that was the land, and exclaiming over the rapid progress they were making. He knew the Admiralty at Queenstown wanted all ships to stay well offshore, but he believed that fussy old Admiral Coke was exaggerating the submarine menace. Certainly they had sunk a few useless old freighters in the past. And of course, the Navy had got a fearful shock when that sub sank the three cruisers *Aboukir* and *Cressy* and the other one, whatever her name was. But the truth was that two of those cruisers were actually stopped when they were torpedoed. Besides, the Navy had no ship as fast as the *Lusitania*. Even at the steady eighteen knots she was presently making, Old Lucy could outrun the fastest submarine. She could almost outrun a torpedo!

As for zigzagging, he had the comfort of his passengers to think of. He commanded a passenger liner, not a destroyer. The Navy boys wouldn't mind the ship being thrown around like a runaway pony, but *his* passengers were just sitting down to lunch. They certainly would not appreciate having their soup tipped into their laps! No, the *Lusitania* would not zigzag to please Admiral Coke. Nor would he order the passengers to don life jackets. Mr Regan had been quite idiotic about that. As if the fact that they did it on the *Mauritania* was likely to convince anybody!

He cast his eye along the boat-deck, where the lifeboats swung on their davits, ready to be launched. Captain Turner was glad he had ordered that precaution, anyway. It was reassuring to the passengers. And at least the crew had been able to accomplish that much without botching it. God help them if they were ever torpedoed. He didn't think they had enough skilled men to launch more than half of those boats. The trouble was, every decent sailor had volunteered for service when the war started. The kind of men that were left were either too old for the Navy, or too worn out, or no good. Captain Turner would not have sailed with most of them if it had been peace-time. Back in those days the great liners had the pick of the crop. Any sailor worth his salt would give an arm and a leg to work on the great transatlantic route, where the pay was good and the conditions were excellent. Those who worked on the great ships like the *Lusitania*, the *Mauritania* and the *Deutschland* were proud of their ships and their achievements. They were the elite among sailors – a kind of aristocracy of the sea. Now he had to be satisfied with the leavings of every port in England and America – half-dead idiots and thieves!

He knew in his heart it wasn't as bad as that – many of the crew were willing and eager to learn, many were competent, and a few of the older hands were prime seamen – but William Turner was a perfectionist, a man who had learned his seafaring the hard way. He knew what the Cunard Line and its passengers wanted. They wanted a fast, comfortable trip. They wanted to be pam-pered. And they wanted to be safe.

Captain Turner intended them to be happy as well. And that was a more difficult proposition.

U-20 was travelling at her top speed underwater. She could not maintain this speed for long, because it rapidly depleted the power in the wet-cell batteries. Nevertheless, Walter Schwieger pushed her as hard as he could. If they could manoeuvre into position and be in the right place at the right time, they would get a clear shot at this liner. One torpedo would slow her enough. She would be a lame duck. Then they could finish her off at their leisure.

Otto Lanz was at his usual post at the plotting table. Walter Schwieger slid into the cramped seat next to him. 'Well, Otto?' he said in a low voice.

'Certainly either *Lusitania* or *Mauritania, Herr Oberleutnant*. I think *Lusitania*. Look at these vents here, yes? On *Mauritania* they are large, proper dorade-style vents. See, *Lusitania*'s look like chimneys. Yes, it is *Lusitania,* I think.'

'How long before we come in range, Otto?'

The chart was spread out on the table, a maze of thin lines and shades to indicate different depths. The Irish coast looked like the wandering path of a spider that had dipped its feet in ink. Otto glanced at the pencil lines that indicated the course followed by *U-20* and that of the liner. 'Ten minutes now, I think. Yes, perhaps ten minutes.' They both looked at the submarine's clock. It was almost two o'clock. *U-20* had submerged at twenty past one.

'*Herr Oberleutnant*, we will give the usual warning, yes?' Otto Lanz was asking him to surface, to warn the ship and give the passengers a chance to escape.

'Don't be a fool, Otto.' Walter Schwieger's voice was low. This was not for the men to hear. 'If we surface she will simply outrun us, you know that. What is the top speed of the *Lusitania*?' He dragged Otto's book towards him and consulted the information it contained. 'Twenty-seven. Twenty-seven knots.' He shook his head. 'There must be no warning.'

Otto Lanz gasped.

Walter Schwieger glared at him. 'We have our orders, Otto. She is a British ship. She is in the war zone. We have published warnings in all the newspapers. They know what they are doing.'

'She carries over four thousand people.'

'She was built as an auxiliary cruiser, yes? It says so here. Look.' He jabbed his finger at the book. 'This is your job, Otto, you know all of this.'

Otto Lanz nodded. 'Too well, *Herr Oberleutnant*.'

Walter Schwieger got up. 'Up periscope.'

He gazed for a brief moment at the oncoming ship, estimating its speed relative to that of the submarine, calculating the course. A seepage of icy cold water had covered the 'scope in beads of cold sweat. He cleaned the glass and peered through it again. Yes, she had not altered course. Incredibly, she was not zigzagging, or taking any precautions that he could detect.

'Down 'scope.'

'We will attack with one torpedo and keep one in readiness.' The order went along the hull. In the torpedo room the men made the last adjustments to the 'tin fish'. Torpedoes were delicate instruments, and needed constant attention to be ready for action. If a torpedo misfired now, or failed to explode on contact, they would lose the best target of their careers. They checked and double-checked everything with extreme care. Then they passed the word that the torpedo room was ready.

'Please, Mother, may I go and watch Ireland from the boat-deck?' Oisín had been planning this little white lie for some time. They were all finished lunch. Mother and

Connie were chatting about the weather. His napkin was full of Cumberland ham, and he had managed to get it inside his jacket.

'Yes, go along and watch for Cork,' Sarah said. 'And no more stories about whales.'

Oisín made his way carefully between the tables, trying to conceal the bulge under his left arm. Once outside, he went straight to the deck where the cabin was. From there, he knew his way down. He swung the heavy steel door back and found himself once again in the darkened stairwell. He began to move down slowly, as before. Once again, he was aware as he passed the waterline of the change of temperature, the condensation on everything. Once again, he had the feeling that he was descending into some dark underwater cave.

'Crumbs, the water must be cold out there,' he thought. 'Icy cold.'

Through the crystal clarity of the eyepiece, the liner looked enormous. She had been painted to disguise her shape, but the narrow hull that was more like that of a warship was a certain give-away. Besides, she had four funnels, and that had to be something very big.

Walter Schwieger was calculating the range. Even though the submarine was warm from the presence of so many men, he felt something cold around his heart. The water seeping from where the periscope went through the steel skin of the hull was getting in his eyes. He had to stop and wipe them frequently.

'Range a thousand metres,' he said. 'Closing.'

Then, shortly, he said, 'Eight hundred metres. Closing.'

Oisín found himself at the bottom of the steps once again. The light down there was faulty, but by its faint and flickering gleam he found the brass wheel that led into the hold. It would not turn. It was stuck. Would he have to give up and return to the deck? Break his promise?

He twisted with all his might and the iron bars ground against the metal of the door and opened slowly. The door swung back and he found himself in the unbearable scream of the turbines once again. He did not close the door behind him in case it might be jammed again on his way back. He made his way along toward the cells.

'Six hundred metres. Closing on a steady course. Stand by.'

The tension in the submarine was unbearable. Everyone was holding his breath. Rueff, on the helm, was gripping it so tightly that his knuckles were white. He was another of Lanz's kind, Walter Schwieger knew. He had made it clear that he was against sinking merchant ships without warning. Walter Schwieger had already made up his mind to have him transferred when they returned to port.

Lanz had broken a pencil and was likely to break another in a moment. There was a wild look in his eyes.

'Five hundred metres. Closing on a steady bearing.'

Now the tension was electric.

'*Los!*'

The hull shivered as the torpedo left its tube, adding its weight to the equation that was the Great War.

Sunday 7 May 1915

Torpedo

A torpedo is a delicate instrument of death. It leaves its tube with the reluctance of a shy person who leaves the shelter of his home to go out into a roaring crowd. Driven forward by two tiny propellers working in opposite directions (for balance), it is powered by nothing more dangerous than compressed air. On its nose is another tiny propeller, which begins to spin as soon as it moves. This is the lock that keeps the torpedo from exploding within the submarine itself. As it spins, it works itself off, and eventually falls away. Now the torpedo is armed, and the three hundred pounds or so of high explosives in its head become its most important component. But if any of those steps fail, the torpedo itself is a failure. It may remain in the tube, unlaunched, and likely to kill its nearest and dearest instead of the enemy. Its compressed air motor may not work, or may work too slowly, and the torpedo will simply drift about like a wounded seagull. It may not arm itself, and the target may feel no more than a slight bump, as though it has struck a floating log.

This torpedo was a good one.

It launched.

It armed itself.

It streaked across the cold green sea, as straight as an arrow. As it went, it left two trails. One, deep down, was the line the torpedo draws in the water from its rushing propellers to the submarine's own tubes. It can only be seen from high above, perhaps from the lookout station of a big ship. The second was the trail created by the spinning of its propellers and the compressed air escaping. This can be seen by something as low as a periscope. It is called the bubble-track and that is what Walter Schwieger watched.

He thought again of the lines drawn on the blackboard in his old school. He thought that this time the equation would add up to something important. In the equation he saw death on a grand scale – something horrific, startling. There were no squalid numbers here – no ordinary seamen who should have known better, anyway. Here were women and children too. He foresaw one or two hundred dead – killed by the explosion, dying of shock, fumbling into the lifeboats and falling over the side. The world would be shocked by these numbers. Also in the equation was glory. Walter Schwieger was surprised to find that he was hungry for that. He saw an Iron Cross in the equation, perhaps with the Kaiser himself pinning it to his tunic. He saw promotion. A long rest.

Walter Schwieger was not good at equations. His schoolteacher was never happy with his mathematics, and in his naval training he was always ahead on tactics, and seamanship, and practical things, but behind in numbers.

He had no idea how destructive his torpedo would be.

How many it would kill. How it would eat his own life as well as the lives of its victims. How few of the things he foresaw would ever actually happen.

On the deck of the *RMS Lusitania*, people had finished lunch. They sat back and patted their stomachs, saying that Cunard really did try in the food department. They were appreciative of the efforts the Line made, scrounging for decent food for them, aware that shortly they would land in a country pauperised by war, where there were shortages of almost everything, including young men of military age. They were dying in their thousands at the Western Front. For example, at the First Battle of Ypres, where Batface's son Donald fell, 100,000 young men died or were seriously wounded. Even as the torpedo made its way towards the *Lusitania*, the second – and bloodier – Battle of Ypres was in progress.

So the passengers were pleased to have eaten decent food. They were thinking ahead, with a mixture of longing and fear, to the home that awaited them a few hundred miles ahead. They were hoping for good news of loved ones, and dreading the black-edged telegram that said that a loved one had been swallowed by the Great War. They were chatting, delaying over their coffee. Or they had come out on the port-side deck to see the Emerald Isle in all its glory on a fine summer's day.

Sarah Moore was leaning on the rail, watching the coastline intently. Connie was pretending to watch the coastline, but was secretly waiting for Tom Boland to emerge from the dining room with his parents. Linda Davis had gone down to her cabin to collect the tiny binoculars called opera glasses. Tom Boland was waiting for a break in his father's flow of talk to ask to be excused so that he could go on deck, and his mother, cured of her seasickness now that they were within sight of land, was watching his anxiety with an amused smile. Batface was swirling a spoon in a coffee cup and brooding on his son Campbell's last letter, the one which mentioned that he was due leave sometime in May and hoped to see his father then. Old Glassy Eye was hobbling along the boat-deck, staring spitefully at a Home-Rule-mad Ireland which did not understand how kind England had been to her. The American, the Harvard professor of Latin, was reading a guidebook to Ireland, a place he hoped to visit before returning to the States. He had just read that the motto on Cork city's coat of arms is *Statio Bene Fide Carinis*, 'a safe haven for ships', and he was smiling because it was a quotation from Virgil, one of his favourite Latin poets. Patrick Regan was on the bridge counting the lookouts and making sure they were doing their job. Captain Turner was finishing his lunch in the captain's day cabin. In front of him was the text of yet another signal from the Admiralty in Queenstown warning of submarine activity in and around the inshore sea lanes of the south and west coasts, and out in the western approaches.

The torpedo was bubbling and drawing its line on the sea. The first person to see it was a young man who pointed it out to his neighbour as a curiosity. He did not recognise it for what it was. It is rare that a man recognises his own death coming to him.

The second person to see it was a lookout, who knew immediately that it was a torpedo. He was high up in the foretop and he could see the double track, the deep one where the torpedo itself was and the surface track left by the bubbles.

He lifted his loudspeaker to his lips and shouted, 'Torpedoes. Two of them. Starboard side.'

All the passengers looked towards the foretop. They saw the lookout standing there. He had gone back to staring at the sea. They looked towards the sea and noticed the thin white line. They looked back to the foretop and the lookout was gone. They blinked, as though they had seen something. They blinked again. Then they looked towards the bridge. Nothing happened. The ship sped on. There was no rushing about. Had anyone heard? Did they imagine it?

'Torpedo! Starboard side!' The voice of a second lookout startled them. And this time something happened. Patrick Regan had rushed out onto the wing of the bridge. He was standing there, shouting and pointing.

Walter Schwieger was watching through his single glass eye, almost a mile away, safe beneath the bright sea. He told Otto Lanz that the shot was accurate. Otto Lanz sat at his navigation table thinking that after all the Greeks captured Troy by a dirty trick – perhaps the crew of *U-20*, too, would one day be heroes.

It was too late for the *Lusitania* to do anything. The lines converged.

Captain Turner had left his day cabin and was standing with his hands on the teak rail that surrounded the starboard-side windows of the bridge. He was just in time to see Walter Schwieger's white line connect with *Lusi-tania*. He felt rather than heard the dull thud of the torpedo, and thought, 'So much for that.' The *Lusitania* was not even checked in her speed. Three hundred pounds of explosive deep inside her belly, and the effect was minimal. Already Captain Turner was thinking that there would be a second torpedo, that he must begin evasive action. He glanced towards the coast and estimated the distance at ten or twelve miles. Not very far. They must make for the Old Head. Patrick Regan turned towards him. There was a wild, desperate look in his eyes. 'Bastards!' he said.

Then the hull was shaken by a second, enormous explosion.

Everyone heard this one.

Walter Schwieger had watched his torpedo go straight to the *Lusitania*'s heart. He saw the plume of water rise and fall away. 'Hit!' he shouted, feverish with excitement. 'Forward of the first funnel.' Then, as he watched for some check in the ship's speed, he was astonished by a second plume, huge, as wide as an enormous oak tree. It rose, full of dark matter and a blue flame, water and steel and other things, and when it fell, he could see a hole like a great door burst outwards in the ship's side by some terrible god, a foaming tide of steam and smoke and dust flooding through it.

'My God!' he gasped. 'What was that?' For a moment, he thought that there must be a second submarine firing torpedoes, but then he realised that the Imperial Navy had not yet invented a torpedo that could cause an explosion as big as that. The great roll of this secondary explosion reached the submarine and the hull became a dreadful drum. They were buffeted and thrown about by hammer-blows.

The man who first saw the torpedo was reeling about, clutching his head. He had been at the centre of both explosions and the change in pressure had damaged his brain. He was like a maddened bull, lunging and stumbling and screaming silently. Old Glassy Eye watched him with horror. His companion, to whom he had pointed out the white track as a curiosity, was dead. Sarah Moore had been knocked down onto the deck by the second explosion. Connie was thrown against a porthole, banging her head hard enough to draw blood. Batface had fallen backwards onto a deckchair and was sitting there like someone relaxing in the May sunshine. Below decks Linda Davis understood the noise and the vibration and grabbed two life jackets from her cabin. She rushed along the passageway, and headed for the open air.

Connie slid down against the wall of the grand entrance. When she reached the deck, she drew her knees up and looked around her. She knew the ship had been attacked. Already she sensed a change in the angle of the deck, and knew that they were sinking.

She saw a group of sailors rushing towards her. At first she thought they had come to pick her up, to stick a plaster onto her head where the blood was coming from. But they stopped at the first lifeboat davit and began to gesture to each other. An officer arrived, and she saw that it was Patrick Regan. He had a megaphone and was shouting something through it. Passengers began to gather around him.

'Quick!' someone said. She felt an arm dragging her to her feet. It was Linda Davis. 'Put this on. Get into the lifeboat.' Linda Davis pulled a life jacket over Connie's head. She pushed her forward in the direction of the lifeboat. 'Hurry, Sarah!' she said. 'Hurry!' The three of them rushed along the deck. The lifeboat was almost full. Patrick Regan saw them and made a hurrying gesture with his left hand. In a moment they were climbing aboard. Linda Davis sat on the far side, with Sarah in the centre and Connie nearest the ship.

'Thank God we're all safe!' Linda Davis said. The sailors began to lower the boat, hand over hand. Suddenly Sarah Moore stood up, a stricken look on her face. 'Oisín! Where is my baby?!'

She began to climb out. A sailor tried to push her back. Hands stopped her. Patrick Regan said, 'Don't get out, missus! The ship is going fast.'

Connie looked along the deck and saw that already the bow was pointed down at the ocean floor. How long had it taken to get to this? A minute, two minutes? The ship had turned slightly towards the land.

'Let me out!' Sarah screamed. 'My boy is still in there!' But strong hands held her. She was drawn back into the press of bodies.

Oisín! Now Connie remembered the pieces of meat. She remembered Oisín telling her one of his incredible stories, something about prisoners, and food, and spies, and art thieves, all confused.

'I know where he is!' she shouted. In a moment she had wriggled out from the crowd. The lifeboat was below the deck level, so she had to stand on the gunwale and step upwards to the rail. She was off before anyone noticed.

'Connie! Come back!' Sarah Moore was on her feet again. But Connie was gone, and Sarah collapsed in tears onto the seat. Linda Davis enfolded her in her arms.

Patrick Regan, standing by the davit supervising the lowering of the lifeboat, watched her slip away from him along the sloping deck. He shrugged. There was nothing he could do now. He could not leave his post to follow her. His eye followed the line of the deck and he noted the angle of inclination. He realised that the ship was still moving at speed, forcing more and more water into the torpedo holes. He thought they had been struck by two torpedoes. He estimated that they had ten minutes. In that time, he knew, it would be impossible to launch even half the boats. Besides, the ship was rolling onto her starboard side. Soon it would be impossible to launch any of the port-side boats. With half his mind on the lowering of the boat, and half on his calculations, he estimated losses of perhaps seven or eight hundred people.

Connie was racing along the steeply sloping first-class passageways. She rounded a corner and ran smack into the portly form of Lord Muck.

'What ho, young lady!' he said. 'Ain't you in a hurry!'

'Out of my way!' Connie shouted. Lord Muck was wide enough to block most of the passage.

'Shouldn't you be going in the other direction?' he asked. But she slipped past him and found the door that led down to the hold.

'Hey! Stop!' Lord Muck shouted, too late. He saw the door swing shut behind her, and shrugged his shoulders. He carried on up the slope of the passage. He found himself in the clear air of an Irish afternoon, a slight heat haze developing along the coast, a glassy sea. He found himself standing beside Batface.

'What you think, eh?' Lord Muck asked. Batface turned a grey countenance towards him. 'Not enough lifeboats,' he said. 'They can't launch them.'

Lord Muck shrugged. 'I can't swim.'

'Nor I,' Batface said.

They made their way together towards an empty lifeboat, still swinging on its davits. They climbed in and gestured to some other people to do the same. After a few moments two sailors came towards them and started to pay out the falls. The lifeboat began to go down towards the sea far below. Now there was a rush of people and the lifeboat filled rapidly. Too rapidly. Soon it was full to bursting. Batface was enraged. 'Get out!' he screamed. 'We're too full! Get *out*!' He began to lash out at those around him. Something had snapped in his brain. He picked up an oar and brought it crashing down on the skulls of people struggling to get aboard. They wailed and covered their heads with their arms. Lord Muck watched him impassively. He brought the oar down again. And again. A glancing blow caught a sailor on the ankle and he let go of the falls of the rope. The bow of the lifeboat dropped suddenly and people began to fall out. Lord Muck was one of the first to go, actually falling outwards as well as down, catapulted by the force of the drop. He plunged into the icy water and vanished from sight. Batface grabbed the seat in front of him and held on. His swinging legs made contact with the bow of the lifeboat and he stood on that. He was aware suddenly of a creaking sound and realised that the lifeboat was swinging on a single rope. Below him, Lord Muck was settling face downwards in the water, his hands flapping ineffectually. He reminded Batface of a wounded duck.

The boat with Sarah and Linda Davis in it had pulled away from the ship. From that distance they could see the tip of one of the propellers just rising above the surface. Sarah was hysterical. She kept trying to jump back into the water.

'Connie!' she screamed. 'Oisín!'

Connie was climbing the stairs downwards to the hold. She was almost upside down. Because of the angle, she felt as if she was climbing along the underside of the big branch of an apple tree in the orchard at Ballyshane. She was totally concentrated on the effort of maintaining her grip. It had not yet occurred to her that in three or four minutes it would be completely impossible to climb back. Nor had it occurred to her that since she had started to climb down, she had made no more than eight steps.

The power went suddenly and the stairwell was plunged into complete darkness. Suddenly she was aware of the moisture that was everywhere, making her grip on the steps uncertain. She was terrified now that she would plunge backwards off the stairs and tumble to her death in the hold.

She realised it was useless to try to go down. Bother Oisín! she thought. He always was awkward. She began to climb back upwards and this was slightly easier than it had been to get down.

She was overtaken by something coming from below. It

brushed past her legs, then her hands. Rats! Another came past. Then another. She felt like screaming but knew it was useless. She climbed steadily. Now the rats streamed past her, coming up from deep down in the guts of the ship, where they lived on the leavings of the world. They are always the first to know when a ship is doomed, a sign to sailors that the case is hopeless.

Connie reached the door again and was about to slip through when she heard something else in the darkness. It was someone cursing. A sailor, she thought, with language like that. Whoever it was, he was cursing the rats. She heard a boot striking metal and the words, 'How's that, you brute?!' There was something familiar about the voice.

'Oisín?'

'There's bloody rats everywhere!' It was Oisín's voice. 'You'd think . . . a ship like this . . . they wouldn't have rats!' The voice was getting closer. 'Hey! Connie!' he shouted, almost in her ear. She felt his hand on her foot. 'Hey! We're sinking!'

They burst out into the passageway and made for the sunlight.

Out on the boat-deck, Old Glassy Eye was screaming for help. Several sailors had tried to persuade her to stop screaming and get into the last safe lifeboat but she was rooted to the spot with terror. Eventually Patrick Regan walked up to her and struck her full on the cheek. She stopped screaming, as though someone had pulled a switch. 'Get into that boat, blast you!' he growled. He pushed her towards the lifeboat and she was dragged in by willing hands.

'Lower away, there! Handy, boys. Steady now.'

Connie and Oisín came rushing along the deck too late. The lifeboat was already too far down the ship's side. The sailors were lowering it at great speed, anxious to find some safety themselves because now the bow had vanished and their feet were sliding on the deck. Batface's dangling lifeboat had been lowered into the sea by the sinking ship. It floated upside down with five people on its back, Batface in the centre.

'Go!' Patrick Regan told them. He pointed towards the mountain that was the stern. 'Get up there, and jump at the last minute. Take this.' He removed his own life jacket and pulled it over Oisín's head. 'Tie the strings, Connie!'

'What about you?' Oisín cried.

'Go!' he shouted. 'Get off, quickly!'

There was no time to climb the deck. Connie took Oisín's hand, and together they stepped off into the sea. As they fell, Oisín saw Sir Hugh Lane step through a door and wave briefly to them. He seemed to be smiling.

SUNDAY 7 MAY 1915

THE EVENING OF A BLACK DAY

A warm darkness settled over the town of Queenstown. Usually on such nights the promenade was full of late strollers – sailors and their girls enjoying the stars, the ladies and gentlemen of the town walking up and down, young men perched on the sea wall fishing for mackerel – and the gentle thud of boats coming alongside and discharging their crew onto the docks would be heard. But tonight the air was electric with shock, and the harbour was full of the streaming lights of trawlers and warships coming from the disaster, and with the uneasy riding lights of those who had already returned and discharged their dead. There were lanterns all along the front, and crowds gathering at every new arrival.

'Has anybody seen ... ?' was the perpetual cry. Old men, young women, children, mothers, fathers, husbands, wives, brothers, sisters, friends. The loss was universal. Even those who had spent the day safe ashore in their homes in the town had lost something – innocence, perhaps. The Germans have sunk the *Lusitania*, they told each other. It was scarcely to be believed. A thousand dead, they said. They shook their heads. They could not think of anything else. They repeated the same things constantly. A thousand dead. *Lusitania* sunk.

The bodies were being laid out in the railway station as they arrived. Lifted from the beautiful sea in all the shapes of death, they lay stretched side by side without distinction, first class with third, third with second, officer and crew and passenger. The stoker lay beside the millionaire. The carpenter was companion in death to the industrialist.

Sarah Moore was stumbling from body to body. She was wearing an appalling bright-red dress lent to her by a portly lady from one of the waterfront bars. She was looking for her children. As she looked into each face and found the eyes, mouth, nose and hair of a stranger she shuddered convulsively, revolted by her own feeling of relief. 'They were someone's children too once,' she kept telling herself. But nothing could stop the relief she felt at finding strange people in those grotesque bundles of death.

There was a child stretched out, as peaceful as if he were asleep, one arm curled above his head. There was a man frozen in the position of a sprinter about to leave his mark. There was a sailor with no face. There was a young man and a young girl clasped in each other's arms.

At the far end of the third line, after she had seen the broken remains of over one hundred human beings, she found the body of Tom Boland. He lay flat on his back, one hand resting on his stomach as though he were about to put it in the pocket of his waistcoat. His shock of black hair lay across his forehead as though his mother had just ruffled it. There was a pool of water behind his head.

Beside him lay Old Glassy Eye, her glass eye gone, the empty socket glaring upwards at the steel girders of the roof, furious to the last.

Sarah Moore was suddenly weak, her legs barely strong enough to hold her up. She tottered sideways and was caught and held by someone who told her to go and sit down, that there were benches over by the wall. A young woman in a three-quarter-length coat, hobble skirt and a large hat with feathers on it gestured to her. Sarah stumbled towards her. 'My children,' she said. 'I've lost my children.' She felt blind, stepping among the bodies, tripping on legs, coat-tails. She found it hard to breathe. She was drowning in grief.

'You poor pet,' the young woman said.

Someone was wailing far up among the last lines of the dead, a high-pitched, desperate wailing that rose into the cold steel girders of the roof and echoed off the glass that was blackened by darkness.

'It's a black day, pet,' the young woman said. 'I never saw the like of it.'

'What will I do?' Sarah said. She put her trust in the young woman as if she had known her since childhood, as though they were old friends. 'Please tell me.'

'Go to the Cunard office,' the young woman said. 'That's where they have the survivors kept.'

'Thank you,' Sarah Moore said. She wanted to shake the woman's hand. The high-cheekboned face was shadowed by the huge hat. Sarah could not see her eyes. She had a small brown paper parcel in her hand, tied up with string. There was a cameo broach at her throat.

'Have you lost someone too?' Sarah Moore asked.

'No, pet,' the young woman said. 'I came down on the train. I was shopping in Cork. I'm from over there.' She gestured at the harbour lights. 'Over the water on the other side.'

The Cunard office. No one could get near it. The crowd was enormous. But someone heard Sarah's cries. 'Make way there!' he shouted. 'This woman is off the *Lusitania*.' The crowd parted in front of her, a sea rolling backwards. The door appeared. She rushed down the open path and through the door.

Inside, the crowd was packed tight. The air was thick with despair. 'Please,' she said.

An American voice said 'Mrs Moore?' It was the Harvard man. 'Are you all right?'

'The children!' Sarah says.

'Oh God!' the man said. 'Here, follow me.' He began to push forward, shouting 'Make way there! Make way there!' He was taller than most, broad and strong. He forged a path to the counter, where the Cunard staff were struggling with two long lists.

'This lady is looking for her children,' the Harvard man said. 'She's from the ship.'

'Name, missus?'

'Moore,' Sarah said. 'The children are called Oisín and Connie.'

The man began to check his list. He began with the list of the dead, his pencil held flat to the page, scanning downwards. He licked his thumb and used it to turn the page.

'What was that name?' another man asked.

'Connie?'

'No. The other one.'

'Oisín.'

'That's it,' the second man said. 'That's a funny name.'

Sarah was about to say that the boy was called after a poem by Mr Yeats, when she realised that she had begun to think of the children in the past tense. The boy *was* called after a poem . . . She burst into tears.

'Easy there now, missus,' the second man said. 'All I want to say is I remember that name. Oisín. That's a name that sticks in a fellow's mind. I made him say it to me three times and I still couldn't say it right.' Someone pushed forward and tried to get between Sarah and the counter. Everyone's distress was urgent. 'Stand back there,' the Harvard man said.

'Made him say it?' Sarah was alert suddenly. 'When?'

'Half an hour ago. He came in on the *Bluebell.* That's a trawler that picked up a lot of people,' he added.

'He's alive?'

The man beamed. 'Alive and kicking,' he said. 'He's in the boarding house up the street. Two doors up.'

'What about a girl?' the Harvard man asked. 'Was there a girl with him?'

The man's face clouded over. 'Sorry, sir. I only remember the boy because of the name.'

As they went through the crowd several people stopped them and shook their hands or patted them on the back. They broke free at last into the clear air of the street. A thin layer of cloud had closed out the stars, and the air was heavy and warm. Boats rocked gently at their moorings, and their lights were like long yellow lines on the water, stretching out towards the shore. Further out there were patches of fog.

Coming towards them was a small knot of survivors. Captain Turner was there, a blanket draped around his shoulders. His eyes were fixed on the pavement and he did not look up as he walked past. Mr Boland was just behind him.

'Mrs Moore?' he said.

'Oh, Mr Boland,' Sarah said, remembering Tom's face, as grey as putty. 'I'm so sorry.'

'Have you seen Tom?' he asked. 'Or Beatrice?'

'I have seen Tom,' Sarah said. 'I'm so sorry.'

Mr Boland swallowed hard and looked away. 'And your Connie? And the little boy?'

'Oisín is safe,' Sarah said. 'I hope . . . oh, I hope . . . '

'Yes,' he said. 'We must hope. But it's a black day. A black day for all of us.'

Oisín was sitting on the steps of the boarding house eating a huge slab of bread and butter and sugar. He leapt to his feet and ran at his mother, throwing his arms around her, the butter and sugar making an extraordinary pattern of gold and silver on her red dress.

'Oh, my boy!' Sarah cried. 'Oh, Oisín! You're safe. You're safe.'

'And you too,' he said.

She stood him down on the pavement. 'Let me look at you. Are you hurt?'

'Not a bit,' he said. 'You should have seen the rats! That ship was full of dirty old rats. And I saw Old Turner going up the street a minute ago. He's not a bad old fellow. Did I tell you I saw the submarine? I saw it before it shot the torpedo.'

'Yes dear, you told me you saw it. That was before lunch.'

'Yes, but I did. It wasn't a whale at all. And I was on lookout and no one took any notice of me.'

A sombre group of sailors went by. One of them had *Lusitania* printed on his shirt. Another wore a naval uniform.

'But have you seen Connie?'

A look of shock passed over Oisín's face. 'Where is she?' he asked. 'Where's Connie gone?'

'Oh no!' Sarah Moore cried. 'Oh my God, no!'

'She was here a minute ago,' Oisín said. 'I bet she's gone back for more soda pop. Look.' He held up an empty bottle. 'We got soda pop from the landlady. I bet Connie's gone for more and she never told me. That's girls for you!'

Sarah was staring at him. 'What did you say?'

The Harvard man began to laugh. It was a ridiculous sound. It came from deep down inside him, a low gurgling, chortling laugh. He tried to prevent it escaping, but could not.

'She's gone off on her own for more pop!' Oisín said indignantly. 'That's not fair!'

Just then, Connie came out carrying a plate of bread and two glasses of soda. The Harvard man gave full vent to his laughter and the laughter turned into tears and all of a sudden he was sitting on the steps where Oisín had been, weeping, with his head in his hands. 'I'm glad they're safe,' he kept saying.

Lord Muck came slowly up the street. Ahead of him

he saw those people he had dined with: that quarrelsome woman and her children and the idiot American crying his eyes out. No backbone, these foreigners. At least they had survived, he thought. Not a great many more had. He had heard someone say a thousand – a thousand people dead. It was unthinkable. No one had ever done such a thing before in the history of the world. He was wondering if it would be possible to get a room for the night. In the morning he would telegraph his man of affairs to have some money sent to a bank here. His clothes were still wet. In his left hand he carried the life jacket that had saved his life. It had washed off the deck as the ship went down, and he, his lungs and belly full of salt water, his heart failing him, had grasped it and held it to his face, and it had kept him afloat until someone pulled him into a half-empty lifeboat.

'Good night,' he said to the Moores as he went past. Only the little boy responded, raising a damned enticing piece of bread and sugar in salute. Lord Muck realised suddenly that he was very cold and very hungry.

'I thought you were dead,' Sarah told Connie, whispering it into her hair as they hugged and hugged. But she was thinking of Tom Boland lying on the marble floor of the railway station, the pool of water behind his head.

'Oh, Mother,' Connie said. 'Where did you get that awful dress?'

'A lady made me change,' Sarah said, surprised that she had been able to do such a thing at all. 'She gave me one of her own dresses because mine was so wet.'

Suddenly Connie gasped. 'My hat!'

'What hat, dear?'

'The hat worn by Billy the Kid. The one Great-Aunt Elizabeth gave me in Boston. I wanted to show it to Tom. I left it in the cabin.'

'It doesn't matter,' Sarah said quietly. 'I'll get you another.'

'But I promised Great-Aunt Elizabeth that I'd take care of it.'

'It doesn't matter, Connie,' Oisín said. 'Have some sense, will you. You can't put a life jacket on over a hat.'

'And where did you go?' Sarah asked Oisín. 'Where did you go after lunch?'

'I was feeding the prisoners,' Oisín said.

Sarah wondered if the boy was mad, his mind touched by the disaster. She would have to see about a doctor for him tomorrow.

'I don't think they could've gotten out.' Tears welled up in his eyes. 'No, I don't think they did. And they weren't spies, or art thieves. They were just nice chaps. It was all a mistake.'

He was thinking of the submarine cold of the cells, the blunt heads of the rivets, the moisture on everything that you touched. He was imagining the hold and the cells and the three prisoners diving down into the green sea, the groaning of the hull, the exploding boilers, the inrush of death. He had heard it all, carried towards him through the water as he floated with Connie.

AFTER THE SEVENTH DAY

Walter Schwieger did not get the Iron Cross for sinking the *RMS Lusitania*. He was given command of *U-88* and he and his submarine disappeared without trace somewhere in the North Sea in 1917.

A major enquiry into the sinking blamed Germany for the 1,195 deaths. No blame was attached to Captain William Turner for his failure to zigzag or stay away from the inshore sea-lanes.

No one is quite sure what caused the second explosion – the one that really sank the ship. Dr Robert D. Ballard, who explored the wreck in a miniature submarine in 1993, believes that explosion was caused by coal gas in the forward coal bunkers, the torpedo explosion being the spark that ignited it.

For anyone whose interest in the *Lusitania* has been awakened by this book, a visit to the Cobh Heritage Centre is recommended. Cobh was originally called Queenstown, and the Heritage Centre itself is the old railway station where the bodies of the *Lusitania* dead were laid out for identification.

The best book on this subject currently in print, and one on which I have drawn a great deal for this book, is *Exploring The Lusitania* by Dr Robert D. Ballard and Spencer Dunmore. Not only does it deal with the tragedy and the current state of the wreck, but it also provides a fascinating insight into life on the great liners.

Lastly, the young woman with the big hat who directed Mrs Moore to the Cunard office was my grandmother, Ellen Brice, who was on her way home from Cork by train on the day of the disaster, and arrived at Queenstown to find the station full of the dead.